Mr. and Mrs. Ari Levinsky Invite You to... the Worst Wedding Ever.

An Arranged Marriage Mafia Romance

Arianna Fraser

ISBN-13: 9798530652882
ISBN-10: 1477123456

Cover design by: Art Painter
Library of Congress Control Number: 2018675309
Printed in the United States of America

To the wise and wonderful Wombatina- Laura is the dearest of friends.

And to the crisis nurseries in my city that care for children when their parents are overwhelmed and in desperate need of help. Proceeds from these book sales will go to help fill their wish lists of much-needed items, like cases of diapers, industrial-sized boxes of goldfish crackers, books, formula, toys, and so much more. And socks. Those kiddos can never hold on to a pair of socks. If you're interested in knowing more, there's information at the end of the book.

Contents

Preface

Mr. and Mrs. Ari Levinsky Invite You to... the Worst Wedding Ever is a romantic comedy. But it is also an arranged marriage Mafia romance, so many of the unsavory elements of organized crime will show up here. There's also scenes of explicit sexual activity between a husband and wife, along with profanity. So much profanity.

If these things offend you, please find something more to your taste but thank you for stopping by. Still here? Great! Grab a glass of wine or a cup of tea and settle in. You're going to love Ari and Heather.

Chapter 1: Wait. What?

In which Heather Stanfield, a nice WASPy girl - and Mafia Princess - is given to Mobster Ari Levinsky to create an alliance with her slimy father's organized crime empire.

"Ma, we're not doing this again." Ari Levinsky was irritably tying his own bow tie, having gently moved his mother's hands away.

"What is 'this', Ari? I'm not allowed to worry about my only child? My precious son?" Sarah was not letting this one go. "You're marrying a shiksa! The woman bearing my grandchildren isn't one of us? How are you planning to raise the kids? She's a Protestant, isn't she? I will not abide this being one of those households that has a Hanukkiah and a Christmas Tree all scrunched up together in the living room!" Sarah's voice was rising, "I won't have it, Ari!"

Finishing his bowtie with a groan of relief, the blond giant turned to his mother. "Ma, you have to sit down, you're getting all upset here." More or less plopping her onto the couch, Ari took a knee beside her. "Didn't I let you plan the wedding?"

Sarah nodded reluctantly.

"You're my queen," he soothed, kissing her powdered cheek. "But you've known Dad had this planned since she was born. We're getting married. In fact," he checked his watch, "I have to head over to sign the *Ketubah* in a minute."

Sarah sniffed, placing a black yarmulke on his head. "But a Protestant! You're marrying out of the faith!"

Her son started laughing, "Oh please, Ma. You were a Roman Catholic when you married dad." Ari stood, so tall that he blocked the light, casting his displeased mother into shadow. "It's not like it matters," he said, straightening his cuffs. "She does what she's told, I get her dad's territory and you get grandkids. Everybody's happy."

***

Everybody except for the bride, of course...
She was sitting in an explosion of chiffon, hairspray, and giggling, staring blankly at a faint water stain on the ceiling. Two days ago, she was in Florence on a college graduation trip with three of her closest friends. And now, she was here in a group of complete strangers who'd look at her, whisper something in Yiddish, and giggle.

It was, apparently, her wedding day.

48 hours ago...
Heather Stanfield never failed to note the irony of Jolly's name, because her father's closest bodyguard never signified anything but dread for her. And here he was, standing in the hotel lobby and looking impatient as she and her friends walked in, giggling a little after a late lunch and a couple of bottles of wine.

"Jolly? What are you-"

Checking his watch, the man huffed impatiently. "Get packing, we have to be on the jet in an hour."

Heather stopped so suddenly that two of the other girls walked right into her. "What are you talking about? I have another two weeks! Dad promised!"

Looking behind her, Jolly nodded slightly to the bodyguard that she knew had been tailing her group for the last five days. The man headed for the elevator and Heather moved faster. She knew that if that creep packed for her, at least one pair of her underwear would end up in his pocket and all of her important things would be left behind.

"I'll do it, Jolly! Just give me a minute!"

The hotel suite was nearly silent as her friends awkwardly tried to help her pack. As far as anyone outside of New York City knew, Heather was the only child of billionaire industrialist Andrew Stanfield- including her college friends, who were getting a sense for the first time that maybe that wasn't the entire story.

The two hulking men crowding her as she zipped her suitcase closed looked like former boxers with repeatedly broken noses, scar tissue around the eyes, and mean-looking. They more or less enclosed Heather between them as they herded her out of the room.

"Can I please say goodbye to my friends?" she begged, but her odd little trio was already halfway down the hall. Waving to her appalled friends as the elevator door closed, Heather slumped against the wall. *Yep, my vacation is officially over*, she thought bitterly, *along with my freedom.*

***

But of course, it could be worse.

"Yes, tomorrow," Andrew Stanfield confirmed, rapidly typing something out on his computer, "everything's taken care of. You just have to show up and look pretty." He still hadn't looked up at Heather, his only child, wringing her hands and standing in front of his desk.

"Wh- are you serious?" she gasped, "I've never met this guy!" This was not completely accurate, she and Ari Levinsky had run across each other at "special events" a few times as children before mob alliances became more ruthless and any occasion tended to end in gunfire. But this was grown-up and terrifying Ari Levinsky, a giant of a man who ruthlessly ruled his mob territory. A simple Google search sent out deeply alarming spirals of information on the Levinsky Mafia. Every media outlet in Manhattan gleefully reported on bodies washed up on shore, horribly mangled, or warehouses set on fire and burned to the ground in seconds. All the details, except for one. That the terrible deeds were ordered by Ari Levinsky. Her completely indifferent father hadn't looked up from his computer monitor once. "Go talk to your mother, she'll bring you up to speed."

"Candy is not my mother!" Heather protested, but she spun and left the study before Jolly could drag her out.

Andrew's fourth wife was actually his daughter's age. He'd met her, in fact, at their high school graduation and their wedding was the most mortifying experience of Heather's life. Until now.

She finally found Candy getting a rubdown from a troublingly attractive massage therapist in her "solarium." And as usual, she knew nothing. Candy's continued good health depended on her ability to know absolutely nothing, and she had to admit, her "stepmother" excelled at it.

"Sorry, girlfriend, I just know we're going to the Four Seasons tomorrow at noon and you're getting married. The announcement's been in all the papers and stuff. *The New York Post* ran it like a funeral announcement, like 'The end to New York's most eligible bachelor'," Candy yawned, checking her phone.

Heather's mouth was opening and closing like a goldfish. "B- but I need a dress and…"

Waving her hand expansively, Candy settled back down under the hands of the supermodel massage guy, who winked at Heather. "Don't worry about it, I guess your husband-to-be is handling everything."

***

She was startled out of her daze by the door abruptly opening, sending all the strange girls into a giggling frenzy. There was a giant standing in the doorway, and when he stepped in, the room seemed to shrink accordingly. There was a bunch of guys behind him, including Heather's father, who was texting rapidly on his phone.

Oh, crap, she thought, *this is Ari Levinsky?*

The handsome fiend was at least 6'4, shoulders broad enough that he'd twisted slightly to get through the door. Thick thighs in beautifully tailored tuxedo pants and he ran an alarmingly massive hand through his hair. It was longer than most mob guys wore theirs, shiny and several shades blonder than his dark beard.

Heather hated guys with beards. They seemed so... unhygienic.

White teeth flashed blindingly as Ari looked around the room, his gaze finally settling on her cringing figure in the corner. "Well, look at you, little Heather is all grown up." There was a chorus of lewd chuckles behind him from his douchey groomsmen. He strode over to her makeup chair, placing those giant mitts of his on her waist and lifting her up off her chair and into the air, level with his grin, her feet dangling. He leaned in, murmuring, "I'm gonna enjoy breaking you in."

Before Heather could even open her mouth to utter some stinging retort that she would no doubt regret, Ari abruptly settled her back on the ground, the jolt clacking her teeth together. With a surprising grace for someone the size of a silverback gorilla, he lifted her sheer veil and draped it over her face. "The *B'deken* is completed," he announced, and the women cheered giddily.

All except one, she noticed. A lovely older woman with silver-blonde hair, two little yappy dogs on her lap, and a deeply discontented glare.

Directed at Heather.

Well, this just gets better and better, she thought, *he just got a round of applause for dumping my veil on my head?* She wanted to ask someone what the hell just happened - wasn't it bad luck for the groom to see the bride before the wedding? Heather chuckled absently as Ari and his Dickhead Posse (and her father, who still hadn't looked up from his phone) headed out the door.

Please, like this whole thing didn't scream bad luck and terrible karmic retribution and utter misfortune. Because she was trying to peel back the veil so it didn't smother her, she missed the moment Ari looked back over one broad shoulder at the sound of her giggle. One dark eyebrow rose with interest, and then he was gone.

The makeup artist took the moment of silence to haul Heather back on her feet. "Take a look!" she urged, "Girl, you look gorgeous!"

Looking in the ridiculously large mirror, angled so every light in the room bounced off of it, Heather squinted. She was tall, 5"8, but anything less than the height of the Statue of Liberty would be tiny next to her groom. Long, thick hair in a sleek chignon, a mix of gold and bronze, and brunette from her stylist who'd gone a little overboard with the highlights. Light green eyes, wide and apprehensive, pale skin. In fact, she suspected her pallor was due to her wedding gown- a gigantic creation from Vera Wang's Fall 2022 line with a billowing skirt of light cream silk and a cinched-in waist.

"You have what is called a 'swimmer's build,' honey," the stylist had told her, putting a knee into the small of a wheezing Heather's back to cinch up the corset. "But this will give you a teeny, tiny waist! You'll look beautiful!"

The white silk corset that went with the dress did indeed give her a lovely, defined waist by folding in her ribs like the rickety legs on a card table.

She put one hand on her hip, the other on the mirror frame for support, trying to drag in a full breath. *They're trying to kill me,* she thought, *I'm going to keel over on the way down the aisle.*

The majestic-looking blonde was rising to her feet, handing off her two little dogs - who promptly tried to bite the unfortunate recipient - and strolled over to Heather and Candy, who had earbuds in and was nodding furiously to some unknown beat. She lightly kicked Candy's ankle, who yelped and pulled out her earbuds.

"Are you-" the woman nodded toward Heather, "her sister?"

Candy chuckled, switching the gum she was chewing from the left side of her mouth to the right. "Nope. I'm her stepmom."

Oh, my god... Heather groaned internally, watching the woman's face pinch like a cockroach had just run over her shoe. "Hi," she put out her hand. "I'm Heather Stanfield." She couldn't stop the humorless little chuckle that bubbled up, "I'm the bride, I guess."

"Well," the woman put one hand on her hip, strolling around her, "I'm Sarah Levinsky. The groom's mother." Stopping her inspection, she leaned in close enough to count the pores on her nose. "You're going to embarrass me, no matter what you do. But here-" she thrust an index card in Heather's hand. "These are your wedding vows. Memorize them."

Heather turned the card one way, then the other. "What language is this?"

"Aramaic," her new mother-in-law said. "You have fifteen minutes before the ceremony begins."

From there, it was a blur. Heather entered the grand ballroom at the Four Seasons, where there was a massive white tent at the far end, surrounded by enough flowers to create its own ecosystem. Random hands pushed her into circling seven times around the blond mobster under the tent, and then he shoved her wedding ring - a gigantic diamond in a platinum setting - on her right index finger. She was given a crystal goblet full of wine to sip and it clinked against her chattering teeth before Ari deftly rescued it from her hand.

The next thing she heard was the crushing of the expensive goblet under her terrifying groom's shoe and the roar of "Mazel Tov!" echoed through the vast room.

Now, *this*, Heather was pretty sure was *not* part of the ceremony. Her girlfriend Mitzie from college was Jewish and she recognized some of these traditions but not the part where this gigantic psycho threw her over his shoulder and walked her from the room, everyone but his mother cheering wildly. One quick elevator ride later and she was soaring across the sumptuous hotel suite and on to the bed, landing hard enough to bounce twice and lose a shoe.

"What are you *doing?*" Heather yelped as he threw up the hem of her skirt, blinding her in white silk. "Aren't we supposed to be- oh! Oh, my god! Downstairs?"

Ari's bristly mouth was currently fastened to her center like a remora on a shark, so his answer was a bit muffled. "Time for the *Yihud*, baby. We got fifteen minutes." And then his tongue went to work on her defenseless clitoris as those tree-trunk arms wrapped around her thighs, spreading her wider.

Heather flailed free of her skirt just long enough to see her legs thrown over her new husband's massive shoulders before she shrieked and her spine snapped into an arch. Ari's beard was rubbing all over her tender lower lips, making them swell as his teeth and tongue were doing terrible things; nibbling and humming as his tongue tunneled up inside her.

When she tried to pull away from this unprecedented oral invasion, he growled - this gorgeous lunatic growled! - and he yanked her back against his mouth again. Fastening his teeth delicately around her clit, he tickled it with the tip of his tongue and suddenly her hands were in his thick, long hair and she was more or less terrified into the hardest orgasm of her life. *Would he bite it off if I didn't come?* she wondered, panting and getting the pale silk of the dress all sweaty.

"Fuuuuck," Ari groaned, head back, beard wet and an odd mix of lust and surprise on his face. Yanking off her undies, he spun them on his thick finger, grinning at her before tucking them into his pocket. Rapidly opening his pants, he said, "Time to return the favor, baby. Open up, here comes Daddy."

Heather stared at the porn star-worthy cock he was presenting her with and briefly looked around the room for the closest exit. Unfortunately, her new husband noticed and one hand slid behind her neck, holding her still. "I know your hair has to stay all pretty for the wedding pictures, but if you don't get to work, I'll take you back downstairs with come running down your dress."

The jovial thug who'd just brought her off in less than five minutes was gone and the tall, terrifying man who took his place was pulling her toward that colossal cock. Licking her lips quickly, she gulped and opened her mouth. The silky tip slid in and she ran her tongue along it, circling the circumcised edge. Ari groaned and his hips pushed forward, his fingers absently massaging her neck. "More of that," he urged hoarsely, and with a sense of self-preservation honed by years of living under Mob rule, she did.

One hand went up to brace herself against his hairy pelvis, and Heather could feel a thick vein leading to his cock throbbing against her fingers. *So that's what's feeding this monster...* she thought, and it was oddly arousing. Sliding her tongue along the bottom of him, she traced that pulsing vein to the end, her head tilted back and her chin resting on his considerable scrotum. It was almost as big a surprise to her as it seemed to Ari, because his other hand smoothed over her jaw, his thumb brushing her cheekbone.

"Look at you taking me like such a good girl," he praised her, voice a little slurred. His hips pulled back then forward again, sending him back down her throat. Heather concentrated on the heft of him- the heat widening her throat. "Or are you a bad girl, huh?" Ari chuckled, "I'm definitely getting the better part of this dea- oh, shit!"

Heather swallowed against him angrily for that comment and his hand on her cheek slipped to her neck, feeling the bulge of him against the thin skin there. With a series of incomprehensible syllables, her new husband came down her throat.

Finally pulling out of her mouth, Ari growled again, one big thumb wiping his come from the corner of her lips and then flopping on the bed next to her. The luxurious room was silent, save the two of them panting like they'd just run a 10K.

As if on cue, there was gleeful knocking on the door to the suite and Heather heard Fritz the Finger (named so because he'd gotten three of his fingers cut off as punishment for screwing up "deliveries") call out, "Hey, boss. Your fifteen are up. Your thirty, actually and your mom's been texting me every five minutes asking if you're dead."

Sighing, her colossal groom stood up and seized her hand, hauling Heather upright too. "Hey, why don't you get cleaned up while I punch Fritz in the dick for interrupting me." Ari punctuated this with a brisk slap to her butt that sparked a yelp from her. Gritting her teeth, she made for the bathroom in a hurry. Maybe she could turn on the water and scream into a towel so that no one could hear her.

Reapplying her lipstick and trying to clean up the mascara smears,

Heather slumped over the counter. This was her life now. Handed over by her slimy dad without a single glance into the possession of this gargantuan, stupidly hot, momma's boy mobster. Before she could even feel sorry for herself, the door swung open, bouncing off the wall.

"C'mon, baby," leered Ari, "let's get this over with so I can fuck you. I wanna take my time with you tonight." He laughed at her alarmed expression as he ran a wet towel over his beard, removing her slick. "I'm gonna miss smelling you right under my nose all night," he said, tossing the towel on the marble counter as she blushed miserably.

Heading back into the soaring ballroom and trying not to cringe at the applause, Heather forced a weak smile. Even with her efforts to "tidy up," she knew she looked like she'd been defiled in half a dozen positions and just barely came up for air. Ari's mother was staring at them both and she Was Not Amused.

"You're late for the *s'eudah mitzvah!*" Sarah hissed, glaring at Heather as if it was clearly all her fault. "Ari, tuck your shirt back into your pants and get up on the dais!"

Ari seized Heather's hand and plowed through the crowd like an icebreaking trawler in the Arctic, shoving people aside and dragging her in his wake. Her father - who was drinking heavily with a bored expression - and Candy were seated at the head table. She attempted to give her a high five.

"Way to go, honey. You climb that man like a redwood?"

Even so, Heather was cautiously beginning to relax as the fish and chicken were served, speeches and increasingly drunken toasts were made. It was becoming less horrible, this marrying of a gigantic, gorgeous lunatic who killed people for a living.

Until the gunfire, of course.

Chapter 2: A Big F*ckin' Mistake!

In which Heather is rather heroic.
Also, Ari shoots people.

Ari had some impressive reflexes, Heather had to give him that. Because when the rapid, percussive sound of gunfire echoed through the cavernous ballroom, he threw over the table, took her arm with one hand and his mother's in the other, and hauled them off their seats and behind the shelter of the overturned furniture. Then, her gigantic new husband stood up with a roar, pulling a gun out of his tux. *Of course*, Heather thought, *of course, he's carrying a gun.*

The beefy lunatic lit up the dais with gunfire, shouting, "This was a big fucking mistake, you motherfuckers! A BIG FUCKIN' MISTAKE!"

Looking to her left, she saw Jolly pulling her father away to safety with one hand and shooting with the other, leaving Candy cowering and covered in the remains of her *sutlach.* "Candy!" she shouted, reaching for her, "Roll under the platform!" Nodding, her classmate/stepmother seized her phone and did a neat barrel roll over the dais, landing with a thump.

To her right, her new mother-in-law was grimly holding on to both her tiny dogs, who were shaking and yapping at the top of their irritating little doggie lungs. "Mrs. Levinsky!" Heather reached out for her, "We have to get under the dais!" The woman wasn't moving, staring at her with wide, shocked eyes.

But then she let out a shriek as a man - one of Heather's dad's, or

Ari's, or one of the bad guys, who even knew - thudded next to her, clearly dead and spraying her with his blood on impact.

Oh, wait. Not completely dead because he reached for her ankle and then Mafia Matriarch Sarah Levinsky was screaming like a buggered goose and kicking fiercely, losing her grip on her vile little dogs who took advantage of this opportunity to leap from her arms.

This set off another round of screaming from her mother-in-law and she groaned, crawling over hastily and, raising one foot clad in a Gucci pump (with a fashionable four-inch heel), she slammed it into the man's wrist. With Sarah free, she pulled her under the dais, but the blasted woman was sobbing, fighting her and reaching in the direction of her fleeing pets.

"My babies!" she wailed, "They'll crush them, they'll hold them for ransom like Lady Gaga's dogs and cut off a toe each day to send to me! They'll-"

Shaking her briskly, Heather shut the woman up long enough to shout, "I'll go find them! Crawl along the wall here- see where Candy is?" They both watched her stepmother's pink-clad butt wiggle briskly as she crawled along the wall, heading for one of the service doors. The girl might only have three functioning brain cells, but they definitely set off a spark or two when her life was in danger. "You follow Candy, hide behind one of the big steel containers and I'll find the dogs." Sarah began protesting again and she squeezed her arm. "I promise, Mrs. Levinsky, now get moving!"

Heather would like to think there was a moment there, a psychic or spiritual connection that they shared. Where they understood each other completely.

Then, Sarah's eyes narrowed and she snarled, "Unharmed, you hear me?" And she was off.

Groaning, Heather gathered her voluminous skirt around her waist and tied it up and out of the way while she edged to the end of the riser, keeping low and looking for doggy feet amongst the racing human ones. Grabbing a piece of chicken from a smashed plate nearby, she took a deep breath and slid on to the ballroom floor. Time seemed to slow down, then speed up. She could hear

Ari roaring profanities and various threats to the wedding crashers and someone must have given him a new gun because he was still firing.

Heather finally spotted the dogs, cowering by an overturned table and mostly shielded by the dead body of - "Jolly?" she gasped. This was serious. This was really, *really* serious because if her father's terrifying wall of muscle was down... Shaking her head, she skittered across the floor like a drunken crab, cringing as someone flew over her head and into the wedding cake, knocking it off the elaborate stand and spraying shards of china plates everywhere. Those horrid purse dogs were still yapping at the top of their lungs and she paused. Was Sarah's approval really worth these bags of fur?

With a sigh, she pulled the chicken cutlet from her sleeve and held it out, wiggling it enticingly. "C'mere, c'mon, you weasels, come here. I've got a treat, c'mere..." The high-pitched barking was slowing down and their tails speeding up with interest, the beasts creeping closer to her. "Good boys," she crooned, "that's good- *ow!*" A hand fisted into her hair and someone yanked her upright. A gun pointed at her temple as the hair-grabbing creep shouted, "Boss! I got 'er!" Several heads turned toward her, Ari's furious and intent.

"YOU LET GO OF MY WIFE MOTHERFUCKER AND I'LL LET YOU LIVE!" he bellowed, but his threats were cut short by someone else letting off a round of automatic gunfire. It distracted the idiot currently gripping Heather's hair, so she shoved his gun arm up with one hand while driving her sharp little elbow into his solar plexus. She was vaguely aware that Ari and various random henchmen were heading in her direction, but this guy was going to shoot her before they could get across the ballroom.

Still clinging to his arm like an angry barnacle, Heather bit him. Hard. Her other hand scrabbled desperately, trying to find a piece of glass or a fork or something when her fingers touched a large shard of a broken plate. It was good-quality bone china, she noted absently, tempered nicely, and capable of a sharp edge. Briefly wondering what pattern Ari's mom had picked out for the two of them (hopefully not Floral Danica, she *hated* Floral Danica) she swung up and stabbed the guy in the shoulder. Blood spurted from his deltoid muscle in a grisly spray, coating the petite pets and soaking their fur. It startled them enough to let go of the chicken cutlet they'd been fighting over and she managed to grab them both.

The gunfire had finally stopped, and over the ringing in her ears, Heather could hear the groans of the wounded and some pockets of hysterical sobbing in the ballroom. There was the faint sound of sirens as Ari's polished dress shoes paused next to her. "Well, look at you, baby! Safe and sound and with ma's dogs?" The beefy lunatic was pretty tidy, aside from some blood staining his white shirt. "You're goddamn perfect in my book!" Ari chuckled as he hauled her upright, ignoring one of the dogs as it tried to bite him. He found a napkin and spitting on it, he attempted to wipe some of the blood off of her face.

"MY BABIES!" Sarah Levinsky was scampering across the littered dance floor, arms opened wide.

Holding his arms out, too, her son tried to be soothing, "Hey, ma. It's okay, safe and sou-" she ran past him and for a moment, Heather thought she was hugging her. Then she realized her mother-in-law was hugging the dogs and she happened to be standing there.

They were snuffling and licking her hands and Sarah didn't seem to notice that they were covered in blood, which was staining the lovely pale oyster shade of her magnificent Hermes suit. But just to keep her calm, Heather assured her mother-in-law, "Oh, that's from the weird guy who grabbed me, oh, and Jolly's blood too, not the dogs, they-"

Oh, no. Where was her dad?

Abruptly shoving the dogs at their mommy, she stumbled in a circle. She wasn't concerned about Candy, that girl could move faster than a rainbow shirt at a Pride festival. For one moment, Heather caught a glimpse of purple- Dad's bow tie had been purple and... Then Ari was blocking her view with his massive chest and turning her around, surprisingly gently.

"Hey, baby. You're gonna come sit over here and get checked out."

"Wait, is that my dad? Tell me! Is-"

Then, it was Sarah Levinsky in front of her, holding her shoulder and cupping her cheek. "Come on, darling, come sit down. Everything will be all right. Just sit down."

Numbly, Heather obeyed her, staring blankly at the blood smears on her new mother-in-law's suit while she spoke to her in low, soothing tones. Dimly, she heard Candy speak through her chewing gum.

"Aw, goddamnit. I look totally ancient in black."

Chapter 3: "Tell Him to Beat Your Cervix Like a Dusty Rug..."

*In which Heather just wants to forget
her really horrible wedding day. Both
Ari and his mother are eager to "help."
In alarmingly different ways.*

Heather was never sure if it was rescuing her yappy little dogs or her father getting shot at her wedding reception, but Sarah Levinsky was surprisingly, shockingly kind. She patted her hands and spoke in low, soothing tones while her new husband glad-handed the arriving police and strolled between broken chairs and the sputtering champagne fountain. No matter how shaken, every guest fawned over him as if getting shot at during the Levinsky wedding put them on Manhattan's A-List.

Well, Heather thought, pushing her hair out of her face, *maybe it did.*

Candy sat with her for a moment, the doctor checking her over. "Sorry, girlfriend," she offered, and Heather just shrugged helplessly in return. She was immediately engulfed in the Stanfield contingent, who swept her away.

Watching them leave without looking back at her once, Heather realized they'd jettisoned her. "Just like Dad," she whispered.

"There's my gorgeous bride!" Ari was on her before she could blink, sweeping her up in his arms. Her head reeled for a moment from being hoisted several feet higher, but wow, those meaty biceps of his made a pretty decent pillow. "Aw, baby," he crooned, fastening his lips to hers and expressing his sympathy through a fair amount of tongue work, "sorry about your dad. But you got me now, honey! I'll take good care of you." The blond giant's voice lowered at the end of that sentence, and she was vaguely horrified to feel a corresponding tingle in her nether regions. "I'm gonna get you out of here," he nuzzled her ear, "this place is a fuckin' dump. We'll go to my place in the city, get you *all* clean."

"Oh, there will be none of that!" The Mafia Matriarch of the Levinsky Crime Family was back and wearing her mantle firmly on that bloodstained Hermes suit. "Ari, the poor girl's father was just murdered! Have some decency!"

The look of incomprehension on Ari's perfectly boned face would have been hilarious in any other case. "What's indecent about a man wanting to comfort his bride? I'm gonna help my pretty new wife get over this whole fucked-up day by-"

Heather was still cradled in his massive arms and kind of impressed that he was still holding her as easily as he did his handgun.

"Ari! I raised you better than this! She's deep into *aninut* and no matter how impressed you might be with that thing between your legs this is not the time to be unleashing it-"

"Ma!" The blond giant was appalled. Genuinely alarmed for the first time this evening. "I'm gonna give my bride the wedding night she deserves!" He glanced down at Heather, sapphire eyes twinkling in what he probably thought was a reassuring way. "Don't you worry, baby. I got you."

"Oh..." she was trying to decide who she was willing to piss off more, Ari or his mother. But she could feel blood and something that she prayed was just wedding cake congealing in her hair. "It's been a big night. Do you think I could get a shower? I don't even care where at this point."

***

"Oh, sweet heaven this is incredible," Heather moaned, leaning against the tile mosaic of the most unreasonably luxurious shower she'd ever experienced. Big enough to bathe the entire starting bench of the New Jersey Nets and all kinds of shower-heads and levers to turn that gave her steam or exotic oils or random fragrances. She'd settled on rosemary to get all the... whatever that was in her hair out and then a vanilla-honey shampoo and conditioner that delicately poured from a copper spigot in the wall.

She'd just stepped out of the shower and into one of the fluffiest, most glorious towels ever spun from Egyptian cotton when she heard Ari and his mother outside the bathroom door.

"Gimme a break, Ma! She probably hated Stanfield's guts! We all hated Stanfield's guts!"

Ari's deep rumble was making her eardrums vibrate, so she moved her ear away from the door. Which was fine, because she could hear Mrs. Levinsky quite clearly. "I brought you into this world, mister, *and I can take you back out.*" The matriarch's tone was low and deadly, which was actually scarier than when she shrieked. Heather jammed her fist against her mouth because the suddenly hilarious image of this blond behemoth's little mother snapping his neck like a twig flooded her imagination and she bent double, trying desperately not to laugh.

There was some rustling and whispering and then a knock. "Heather dear? It's Mrs. Levinsky. Can I come in?"

"Yes ma'am," she mumbled, throwing on the huge robe she found on a hook by the door. By the way it was puddling around her feet and nearly wrapping around her twice, it had to be her new husband's.

Sarah had a smile for her, so she assumed her mother-in-law was still feeling all soft about her saving those yappy little dogs. "I brought you something for your nerves," she said, offering Heather a little cup with two pills and a glass of water.

"Oh, thank you, Mrs. Levinsky, that's... uh, what are those?"

"Oh," she made that little wavy hand motion people did when something was No Big Deal. "Just something I keep in case of stressful situations. You'll be able to sleep better."

Smiling at her new mother-in-law nervously and then at those mysterious pills, Heather wondered if that initial goodwill from risking her life to save those vile little dogs had worn off. "I don't do so well with medication," she lied, "I just start throwing up all over the place."

That did the trick. Sarah's warm smile faded into a pinched effort to still appear pleasant and Heather sagged in relief. "Oh, my. Well, I'll just leave them with you. And your overnight bag is in the guest room. I'm sending up some dinner because I'm sure you haven't eaten all day."

Absurdly touched by her thoughtfulness, Heather almost teared up. "Thank you, I haven't had a single bite."

"Good," Mrs. Levinsky smiled as she left, "eat some dinner and take those pills. Really. You'll feel better."

Slipping the medication into the pocket of the bathrobe, Heather walked into the guest room, snickering a bit at her mother-in-law's pointed placement away from the master bedroom. At this point, she was more than happy about it. The adrenaline had worn off and she just wanted to lie down. The room was huge, with a big, comfortable bed piled high with silky pillows and quilts in blue and green. There was a soft chair in one corner with a reading lamp and an overstuffed bookcase, and a luggage rack holding her overnight bag

Opening the leather case, she groaned to see the skimpy lingerie that her dear, *dear* stepmother must have packed. It was totally her sense of humor- a hideous, itchy teal lace g-string and a tacky bra with pink puffballs sewed on each cup like perverse, fluffy nipples. Oh, and a note. It was on the fancy engraved Stanfield stationary and in Candy's sloppy handwriting.

Hey, girlfriend.
You tell that man to beat your curvix like it's a dusty rug. He looks like

he's equipped for it.
Luv, Candy

"It's spelled cervix, you moron," she groaned, kicking the vile pile of lace and the note under the bed. There didn't seem to be anything else in her overnight case but a toothbrush, so she vowed to stay in Ari's robe.

Crawling into bed, Heather used her phone to look up the identity of the pills Ari's mother had tried to slip her. "Ambien, with a dosage high enough to roofie a horse. Nice." She flopped over, looking for a cool spot on the pillow. "She probably thought Ari would leave me alone if I was unconscious." Pondering if that would actually stop the man she'd met today, she fell asleep.

***

Later that night...

Sitting upright with a barely concealed shriek, Heather looked wildly around the room, trying to remember where she was and why nothing looked familiar and-

Oh, yeah. Her Dad gave her to another mobster and then got killed and here she was. Stupid, fat tears were running down her cheeks and she'd barely smothered another pitiful sob when her door slammed open.

Ari strode into the room, gun in hand but lowering it when he looked at her sad self huddled on the bed. He was wearing nothing but a very tight pair of Calvin Klein boxer briefs and the look of him was so startling Heather actually stopped crying.

The gigantic lunatic she was now married to was... crap, he really was gigantic. His body was like some X-rated study Michelangelo would have preferred to sculpt instead of that tiny-penised David. He was all golden, tanned skin over sculpted muscles. And hairy.

She'd always dated nice, smooth-skinned boys. Lean, swim team kind of guys with good manners and who took her on nice dates to their parent's country club. Nice boys who made her husband look

like an ogre from the fairy tales. A hot, muscled, sexy ogre.

Then he opened his mouth and proved it.

"Shit, baby- you okay? You were screaming like someone stuck a dick up your ass, and I know it wasn't me, so..." Ari chuckled, casually putting the safety back on the alarmingly huge gun he'd been waving at her. Taking another look at Heather's tear-stained face, he seated himself on her bed and then her on his lap, straddling him before she could put up a fight.

"You look great in my robe, honey," he gloated, running his giant paws over her chest, pushing the fine cotton robe ahead of his rough fingertips. She was squirming, trying to find a place to put her hands that would not be on him, but his giant body took up the entire bed. The robe slid to the edge of her shoulders and she crossed her arms, trying to keep her breasts covered. A slow grin went over that bearded face, teeth flashing white as his gaze was trained on her chest. "You're not wearing anything under this, are you, baby?"

Still squirming, she managed to grit out, "H- Heather. My name's Heather."

His gorgeous face managed to still look gorgeous while also clueless. "Yeah. I know?"

"You keep calling me 'honey,' or 'baby,'" she said, refusing to look him in the eye, worried she'd get all distracted because the man had some serious B.D.E. going. "I just wondered if you knew my real name."

Ari was busy running his fingertips over her collarbones, so she didn't think he was listening. But then he gave her a grin that looked like he was attempting to be soothing. "You're tense, *Heather*," he emphasized. "No wonder, huh? That was a hell of a day, getting married, those trigger-happy motherfuckers-"

"My father dying," she interrupted.

"Yeah, that," the blond giant agreed. "You know what you need, honey? You need to relax. Get rid of some of this tension that's got you all backed up." His hands were on her waist now, lifting her easily up, his biceps bunching as he re-seated her straddling his waist and chuckling when she gasped and tightened her thighs, trying to keep from sinking down on that toned pile of muscle and fur. "How are you gonna get any sleep when you're all pent up like this?"

"I'm really not tense," she gabbled, "I'm really just fi- Oh, my god!" The robe was open and slipped down to her elbows, her breasts bare and despite her best efforts to appear like it was possible that she was an adult, Heather burst into tears again.

"Oh, shit," Ari said uneasily, suddenly seeming to not know where to put his hands. Pulling his head back, he looked down at her tear-stained face. "Yeah, this was a big day, huh?" He winced a bit as Heather tried to speak, then broke back down into broken sobs. The terrifying Mafia King Ari Levinsky slowly put his long arms around her, feeling her shoulders shake with the force of her weeping. He tried patting her back, but the impact from the first attempt sent her into a coughing fit that lasted several minutes.

"Sorry," Heather wheezed, "I think my lungs are just trying to fluff back up from being laced into that corset all day." To her shock, Ari sat very still, holding her like the slightest flex of his monstrous biceps would crush her. Which was possible.

When her weeping dribbled into shudders and finally, small sniffs, Ari pulled up the covers over her slack body, "Get some sleep honey, you got a big day tomorrow."

"Oh?" she barely got the words out, "What's... uh..." dozing off made it difficult to finish the question, but her terrifying new spouse just chuckled.

"Our honeymoon, baby! You're gonna love it." As Ari was leaving, he looked back one more time, winking. "And I'm gonna fuck you so hard you won't be able to think of anything else." With a chuckle that was far more sinister than soothing, the door shut and she was left in darkness.

Chapter 4: A Funeral and a Honeymoon

In which there is actually something worse than Heather's wedding. Her father's funeral.

Andrew's funeral.

Every time Heather thought her life couldn't turn into a bigger disaster, her dad was there to holler "Au contraire, ma petit chou!" Because Andrew was totally a dick like that.

The funeral of Billionaire Philanthropist (oh, god she laughed until she was cramping when she read that gem in the funeral order of service) Andrew Stanfield was a Who's Who for suck-ups and wannabes. Heather recognized a lot of the same faces that attended her disastrous wedding, and she wondered how many were wearing bulletproof vests under their black cashmere coats. Yet they still showed up.

"How many of these people owe you," she murmured, knowing her gigantic husband would lean into her, casting a shadow from his sheer size and bulk, a waft of his Hugo Boss cologne tickling her nose before he half-shouts in her ear.

"What, baby? Who owes me what?"

Heads turned in their direction and she closed her eyes and sighed. He's got her hand - the one wearing his garishly gigantic diamond - pulled into the crook of his arm and resting on a bicep the size of a hubcap. But it didn't matter if her eyes were open or

ARIANNA FRASER

closed, she'd be towed along in the wake of USS Levinsky.

But Ari actually stopped for a moment and the entire procession heading into Green-Wood Cemetery ground to a halt, too. Placing a big paw on her cheek, he tilted her head up to look at him. "What did you ask me, honey?"

Making an awkward glance over her shoulder at the confused line of wealthy New Yorkers behind them, Heather cleared her throat. "It was just a little joke. I was just wondering how many of these people owed you something. I didn't think we'd get this kind of attendance after the shootout at the OK Corral that was our wedding reception."

He's laughing by now, the hearty chortle echoing over the silent lawns of the graveyard. Ari wraps his arms around her in a hug and it's like wrestling a bear. "Baby, I own these bitches! Every one of them!"

Heather's face was half-buried against his chest but she looked back to see the Mayor of New York City, whose head was inching into his neckline, like a turtle retreating into its shell.

As the minister was droning on about her father's "eternal rest," she looked around the rolling hills of the cemetery, the gothic towers, and walls. So many famous people were buried here, Leonard Bernstein, Jean-Michel Basquiat.

And now Andrew Stanfield, whose casket is currently covered by the wailing form of his widow, Candy. She's stylishly outfitted in an ebony Prada suit, complete with a big black hat and a veil. Her form was good, Heather had to admit, prostrate with grief and crushing the flowers on top as she sobbed loudly, "Come back to me, Andy! Don't leave me in this cold cruel world alone!" Two of the Stanfield bodyguards briskly lifted the distraught widow off the coffin so it could be lowered into the ground.

Unfortunately, they put her next to Heather, and Candy leaned on her heavily, lamenting loudly in her ear, "If only he'd given me a baaaabeeee!"

Heather realized that her heels were beginning to sink into the sod from their combined weight at the same time Ari seemed to notice she was getting shorter. Bodily lifting Candy in one arm, he slung the other around her waist and hauled the two of them over to the gravesite.

"Throw some dirt in, baby, we got a funeral reception to get to."

When Heather heard the "clunk" from the handful of clay she'd thrown hit the casket, it finally hit her.

Andrew was really gone. Sure, he'd been a terrible father since her mother passed away when she was ten, but before he sold her off to the Levinsky Mafia, he'd given her a good education, a chance to see the world.

And he was all she'd had.

While her new husband got a big mark in the "Decent" side of her mental ledger for not getting all pissy about postponing their honeymoon for her father's funeral, when Ari attempted to cheer her up that night with his platinum-level oral ministrations, Heather pushed him away. Throwing all sense of self-preservation right out the window, she shoved her murderous groom away from where he'd been yanking down her Stella McCartney pencil skirt (in the custom onyx silk style).

He was not happy. "Did you just tell me no?" Ari snarled, rising over her, looking furious and magnificent because his crisp white shirt was open and she could see those tan, hairy pectorals flex and swell with his anger.

Fruitlessly batting away his giant hands, Heather hissed right back at him, "Yes! Ari, this has been a horrible week for me! My father's dead and I'm not in the mood right now!"

Unfortunately, her gigantic husband chose to focus on a different part of her statement. "This is a shitty week? The week we got married IS A SHITTY WEEK? WHO DO YOU THINK YOU'RE TALK-ING TO, YOU UNGRATEFUL LITTLE-"

"**ARI!** Sit down and shut up!"

The strident order from Mafia Matriarch Sarah Levinsky silenced the roar of her son as if she'd casually reached out and clicked off his volume knob. Since as far as Heather knew, Ari only had two settings - loud and incredibly, painfully loud - this was a miracle.

The only sound left in the guest room was her sniffles, which she was valiantly trying to smother.

"Oh, dear." Mrs. Levinsky shoved her hulking son out of the way and sat down next to her. "This has been an overwhelming week, and of course you're upset! I'd wondered when your father's... ah... passing was going to catch up with you."

Heather knew she was staring at her, jaw dropped and looking - no doubt - remarkably simple-minded, but she couldn't help it. Some saint had entered the fierce, tiny body of her mother-in-law and she looked... kind?

"I'm sorry, Mrs. Levinsky," she sniffled, "I just-"

"You're terribly sad and upset and my son has been attempting to help you work through your grief by sneaking into the guest room every night."

The bedroom was silent except for the clicky noise in Heather's throat when she tried to swallow.

"Of course I knew," she said, taking her hand and patting it. "Now, the two of you will go on your honeymoon tomorrow and have a nice time. You'll be away from Manhattan and all this nonsense. When you come back, I'll be back in my own home and you two can start your lives together. You're a good girl, even if you're a Shiksha and I know you'll make my Ari happy.

"And I..." she gave her huge son a slitted eye glare that clearly threatened death and ruin. "I have raised a good man who will treat you well. Now then!" Sarah stood, clapping her hands together briskly. "Everyone to bed! Tomorrow's going to be a big day!" Giving them both a brisk kiss on the cheek, she ushered her stunned and silent son out the door.

"Wh- what just happened?" Heather asked the silent room.

But as she decreed, the saint currently inhabiting the body of her mother-in-law waved goodbye on the front steps of Ari's stately brownstone the next morning as their ride - the standard, sinister black luxury SUV - pulled away from the curb on the way to the private airport next to LaGuardia.

"Your mom is... wow," Heather tried to phrase it gracefully, "when

she puts her foot down..."
Ari chuckled, the smile curling those plump red lips of his, "Yeah, baby. You do not fuck with Sarah Levinsky," he took her hand, kissing her knuckles with only a little bit of tongue thrown in. "I have strict instructions to..." he rolled his pretty blue eyes elaborately, "wine and dine you and treat you like a lady." Dropping his huge paw to her thigh, he squeezed it meaningfully.
"And then I'm gonna fuck the shit out of you."

***

"Oh, my god," Heather sighed, "this is worth the fifteen-hour flight!" *And the two stops to refuel and the sixteen times Ari almost got my undies off*, she added silently. She was initially politely un-enthused when her new husband informed her that they would be honeymooning at the Port Sudan Diving Resort. In Ethiopia. Not that she was complaining, but her best college friend Madison went on a tour of Europe for her honeymoon, and Marlie from her spin class described a honeymoon stay in a luxury treehouse in The Amazon rainforest that sounded pretty amazing.
But the closest Heather had ever been to Africa was Morocco, and that was because Andrew had a sudden hankering for a Kefta Ta-gine that could only be found at a tiny family restaurant in Tan-gier, so they'd flown there on his Learjet 75 Liberty. (She found out later that her father was also cutting a deal for a shipment of surface-to-air missiles with the owner, but the tagine really was delicious.)
And now that she was here, and the water was an exquisite, crys-tal clear shade of cyan, and the resort really was rustic and lovely, she smiled up at Ari happily. "Thank you, this is so beautiful."
The grin he gave back was truly alarming. Enormous, like him, and showing way too many teeth.
"This is gonna be the best ten days of your life, baby."

Heather would have liked to exclaim about the charming cabana built on stilts in the water with its own private dock. She could have praised the rustic furniture carved from shining wood and

ARIANNA FRASER

the palatial bed, a four-poster draped with filmy white netting and gloriously soft, pale linens. If her new husband's tongue had not been in her mouth, she might have sighed with happiness over the huge, white porcelain tub sitting on an open-air platform overlooking the ocean, big enough even for a foul-mouthed, lumberjack-sized lunatic like him.

Yes, all those things would have been noted and deeply appreciated. But she'd been picked up, and in a move reminiscent of her wedding day hurled across the room to land unerringly on the bed. And her gluttonous spouse had her skirt flipped up over her face and her undies torn clean off before she had the chance.

Ari's bearded face was back between her legs and latched on to her clit like a barnacle before she could whine, "Hey! I really liked those panties!"

So instead, what came out of her throat was a cross between a steam whistle and some kind of chirrup and it seemed to just spur her husband on.

Growling, he rubbed his whiskered chin against her center, scraping the tender entrance and making her thighs attempt to slam shut. "I wish I could get my whole fucking face up you, honey," he growled, diving back in to thrust his tongue into her channel as far as it could go. She could feel the diabolical thing wiggling and setting off sparks that made her hips start rotating in some kind of assistive figure eight, trying to make that tongue brush something, or lick a certain spot or...

But in the meantime, his well-formed nose was nudging against her clit, baring the defenseless little thing and so by the time his tongue left her passage - replaced by two of his fingers and hey, that was a stretch - and that tongue started lashing her clit, she was dragged kicking and screaming into the first orgasm of her honeymoon.

That heartless swine stayed right where he was, calloused fingers scraping her G-spot and his tongue batting her clit like it was a birdie and he was playing badminton with it.

"Please, please stop Ari- please?" Heather's plea for mercy was coming out in between desperate, heaving breaths so maybe he

29

didn't hear her, because it all started again.

"Can't do that, baby," he said, the sound muffled because he was licking between her slick lower lips and making the whole thing a mess. "Gotta get you ready for my cock."

Her hands, pulling at his messy blond hair and trying to dislodge him from her lady garden paused. He had a point. Sure, she'd had that alarmingly large cock of his in her mouth, but she'd only managed to swallow down maybe half of it and she had no idea how Ari's most prized possession was going to fit in the space his fingers were currently occupying.

So when he fastened his lips around her clit and began shaking his head, growling like a dog and pulling on it like a chew toy, her orgasm tore through her. Her legs were over his broad shoulders and she was kicking his back mindlessly, trying to come down from wherever he'd flung her.

"…There ya go, honey. You back with me?"

It was that… that stupid, self-satisfied chuckle of his that brought her back to her senses. Clumsily pushing his wet, bearded face away from her, Heather managed a slurred, "Uh-huh…"

"Good," he growled, "I been waiting for this for a fucking week! Even with coming in that sweet mouth of yours every night and jerkin' off three times a day, it's been killing me, knowing you were right down the hall…"

Ari was leaning closer now, pupils blown wide and almost purring, "Knowing that tight little cunt of yours was just waitin' for me? Goddamn, woman! I thought my dick was gonna explode!"

"You sweet…" Heather was still trying to catch her breath, "you sweet talker, you."

He reared up on his knees, sitting back on his heels and spreading her thighs wide, huge, rough hands stroking up and down the thin skin there. His thumbs moved up to spread her wide, and he groaned happily. "Look at that pretty pussy. All mine."

It was the broad head of his cock entering her that really snapped Heather back into reality. "M- maybe I'm not ready yet, Ari, maybe you're right-"

"Yeah you are," her gigantic husband soothed her, "you're wrapping so sweet around me." His head dropped back and she got to admire him for a moment, the sheer *size* of him, his sharply defined six-pack rippling as he pushed inside her, biceps flexing, and those huge mitts of his squeezing her behind, lifting her to meet his thrusts until he was fully inside her. Heather's severely overtaxed clit was mashed against his hairy pelvis and he'd looped her legs over his elbows, watching his cock slide in and out, getting slicker and shinier with each pass.

"You are so perfect, ba- Heather," he groaned, and she paused. Just the fact that he'd remembered to say her name made her realize the beefy psycho really was *here*, in this moment with her. Really with her.

Gulping, she tightened her thighs around that perfectly tapered waist of his and said, "Why don't you show me what this jumbo-sized dick can do?"

Oh, he showed her. Ari really showed her. He started slow and built momentum until he was pounding into her, pushing her incrementally across the vast plains of their nuptial bed until she was moaning shamelessly, holding up her arms in a plea for him to get closer instead of looming over her like some colossal incubus.

Pushing her legs up against her breasts, ankles around her ears (thank you, Miss Willow's hot yoga class!) Ari put his face to hers, mauling her lips with the same enthusiasm he was expending down below, and it was... wow, it was amazing.

Heather never knew sex could be like this, warm and messy and with laughing and kissing. That he would whisper all kinds of filthy stuff in her ear - highly appreciative commentary about her "tight ass," and how "that juicy cunt is strangling my dick," and "I'm gonna stick my face between your perfect tits and live there," and that she would love it. So much that she jumped right in and whispered dirty little thoughts about what she wanted him to do to her next, and then that apparently set off some kind of starter pistol because they were both barreling towards their finish and-

Then, that magnificent giant who'd made her marry him leaned in close and whispered, "Come all over my cock, Heather. Soak me."

And with a wanton scream like she'd never thought would leave her good girl lips, she did. And then she was flooded with heat and everything was a mess and they were laughing.

Ari pulled Heather up to sit in his lap, still attached to his oversized cock, and wrapped her legs around him and his arms around her and he squeezed her tight enough that she was pretty sure the imprint of his chest hair was tattooed onto her breasts.

And she was okay with it.

Chapter 5: Ari Punches a Shark

In which there is a real threat that Heather may be walking bowlegged for life, and that gigantic, gorgeous bastard she's married to doesn't seem to have a problem with that.

The sun rose over the waters of the Red Sea, which really was not red, Heather thought as Ari railed her from behind. "In fact, the Red Sea gets its name from the occasional blooms of cyanobacteria algae, which upon dying turns the intense turquoise water a rust color..."

"What's that, babygirl?" her hulking groom inquired.

"Oh!" She yelped as he gave a particularly enthusiastic thrust. She hadn't noticed she'd spoken out loud. "N- nothing, just- omigod I think you're going to come bursting through my chest like that thing from *Alien!*"

Most men would be insulted by having their cock being compared to an acid-dripping embryo that tears through the chest of their victim, but Ari merely chuckled as he thrust faster. They were on their balcony, facing the sunrise. Well, Heather was facing down, looking at the water, bent in half, and held in place with her arms straight behind her and the giant currently mauling her senseless, grasping her wrists and pulling her back and forth on his admittedly impressive cock.

He was, in fact, admiring it, slick and shiny from pounding into her with enormous enthusiasm. This was a testament to his oral skills because he'd been going at her for most of the night (she thought, she wasn't sure because time passed differently when perched on the monstrous dick of Ari Levinsky) and this was maybe the fifteenth position he'd contorted her into.

"Aw, honey, you gonna come for me again?"

"Is- is that a trick question?" she wheezed, feeling the silky tip of his cock rub against her cervix.

Ari's enormous paws slid to her waist, "You gettin' tired, bunny?"

That was another thing. This nickname? Better than the generic 'baby' or 'honey,' she guessed. But when he first called her that, she'd asked him why.

"Because when we're fucking and you're gonna come?" Ari's broad chest jolted against her as he chuckled, "Your nose twitches like a bunny's. It's fuckin' adorable."

At that moment, Heather vowed to put Ex-Lax in his coffee.

But now he'd lifted her onto a pretty little table designed for a small plate of treats, perhaps a couple of champagne glasses. Instead, it steadied her back as he looped her knees over his elbows and began thrusting so vigorously that she could feel one of the legs on the table loosen ominously.

But the worst part? The worst part was this heartless, gorgeous lumberjack-looking guy knew she was about to come again. So, it was a race between her crashing into an orgasm or on to the floor if the table gave way.

Throwing her legs together and over one shoulder, Ari grinned down at her, white teeth flashing in his dark beard. "Takin' me so good, bunny." His raspy thumb was circling over her clit, nudging it gently. "Taking all of me. I wasn't sure the first time we fucked if I was gonna get my dick all the way in..." He did some swiveling thing with his hips and she shrieked, legs beginning to tremble. "Just like that, bunny," he chuckled triumphantly, "come for daddy."

***

"So, where'd you go to college?"

"Huh?" Her eyes barely opened to see the long angle of the sun over the ocean. Late afternoon. "How long was I asleep?" Heather groaned, rubbing her eyes.

Her gigantic, diabolical husband had maneuvered her onto his lap on the bed, her butt nestled into his crotch, long, long legs bracketing hers and her head pillowed on his wide, hairy chest. She could feel the rumble of his voice vibrate against the thin skin of her cheek. "Couple a hours. I think you might've passed out on that last round." Ari chuckled heartlessly at her groans. "It's okay, bunny," he soothed, "I got you all cleaned up and put somethin' on that tight little pussy. Looks a little sore."

"I just…" Heather did not know how to handle this beautiful lunatic. He was crass. He talked about all her girl parts and insisted on examining them closely. At length. One of his giant paws was always roaming on some part of her, the sheer bulk of him enclosing her completely. The lines of where her body ended and his began were getting blurred. "You asked me something about school?"

"Yeah," Ari paused to pour her a glass of juice from a pitcher by the bed, helping her hold it until her hands were steady. "Just trying to piece together what I know about you. You went to some boarding school, right?"

Slowly sipping the pawpaw juice, she nodded. "I went to the Emma Willard High School in upper New York State."

His calloused fingers were stroking up and down her arm. "You come home for the weekends?"

"Oh, no. Some weeks in the summers. Christmas."

His hum rumbled against Heather's back. Ari shifted slightly, and she could feel his hip bones press against the soft flesh of her behind. There wasn't a part of her that wasn't engulfed by this mobster who'd married her. "So, you didn't see a lot of your dad, huh?" His whiskered chin brushed her cheek when she laughed a little bitterly. "Some weeks in summer. Christmas." Her hand rested tentatively on his thigh, thick with muscle, sculpted and hard.

"What about college?" Ari rumbled.

"Really?" Heather laughed, uneasily feeling his cock starting to swell against her back, "What's next, my favorite color?"

Ari's giant mitts scooped under her butt, lifting her slightly. "Okay, I'm gettin' hard again anyway."

"Wh- wait!" she gabbled, "The Sorbonne in France! I studied there. Linguistics." He'd turned her around by then, spreading her thighs and settling her more snugly against that endlessly hard dick of his.

Pushing her juice glass to her lips, Ari rumbled, "Keep drinking, your blood sugar's gonna get low. No shit about the linguistics thing? What languages do you speak?"

"Um, Serbian, Macedonian, French, Italian. Uh..." His hips- those snake hips of his were moving again and her sore girl parts felt sort of like how screaming for help would sound. "And- and Russian. I spent a year there, in Moscow."

"Well, look at my genius bride," the grin he gave her was not caring, or gentle. Neither was the next round of extremely vigorous sex he gave her then.

Still, after a suitably romantic dinner, (aside from that scary as heck fried fish, Asa, served whole with its little jagged teeth poking out like she had a Piranha on her plate) that was served on the little terrace of their ocean cabana, Heather's alarming new husband put her to bed and strolled off into the other room to, "Make some calls. I gotta check on those assholes every day or they fuck something up."

They both went scuba diving the next day, and she was in heaven. They explored the Wreck of the Umbria, a ruined ship turned into an underwater castle covered in coral. Ari tugged on her hand, pointing to a stately armada of manta rays, and Heather - very carefully - swam alongside a couple of docile whale sharks.

"How was it?" Asim was their boat captain and an "old friend" of Heather's husband, who was currently peeling off his wetsuit, leaving miles of tanned, hairy skin and muscle on display.

"Yeah, it was great," Ari was now completely naked on the boat deck and indifferent to the gaping stares of three boat hands. "So many whale sharks this time!"

"Tell me, Mrs. Levinsky," Asim had turned to her, "I beg you to tell me that this man did not punch a shark this time?"

Heather started laughing until she realized he was serious. "What, are you kidding? Ari punched a shark?"

Their boat captain was bent nearly double, just howling at the memory. "He did. He punched a shark on the jaw last time I took him out on a dive. He punched a shark in the face!"

Once Heather started laughing, she couldn't stop, either. The colossal, muscle-bound maniac she was bound to - well, for the rest of *her* life, anyway - punched a freaking shark?

"He was lookin' at me!" Ari snarled, pulling on some shorts - no underwear, she noticed - "You can't let them get away with shit like that."

That did it. She was rolling on the deck of the boat, wheezing and wondering if she'd dislodged something internally from laughing so hard.

But the next morning, Heather's gigantic, shark-punching spouse sent her out on a dive alone. "I gotta work, baby," Ari said, guiding her down the dock to the dive boat. "Asim and one of his sisters or cousins or aunts or someone are gonna dive with you. There's a huge coral reef, barracudas, and hammerhead sharks..." He looked down at her, stern behind his Gucci sunglasses, "Don't start any shit about the sharks! Not even a smirk or I'll make you wear a vibrator at dinner. And we have guests."

She shook her head vehemently at the vibrator threat and backed down toward the boat, nearly tripping and falling off the dock. Sliding an arm around her waist, Ari pulled her hard against his pelvis and kissed her soundly. "That's my good bunny," he rumbled in her ear.

Oh, for god's sake, Heather thought, *he's hard again?"* She was still walking bowlegged from this morning, so she almost scampered for the boat.

But Asim didn't seem in any big hurry. He'd sent his deckhands off to get some supplies in a storage unit in the resort, and he took his sister (or cousin or his aunt) and stepped off the boat. "Will you be all right for a moment?" he asked, "I must get a different regulator and a couple of new tanks."

"Oh, no problem," Heather said. She'd just put her oxygen tanks down next to her seat, and there was another entire rack of tanks just across the deck, but maybe they weren't filled. "I'll just go over the dive map."

"Very good," he nodded, and he headed up the dock and onto the beach.

She could just see Ari at the top of the sand dunes, talking on his phone, pacing back and forth.

"You got her?"

"Yeah, Mr. Levinsky, the rifle scope's centered on her tanks. One bullet and she goes sky high."

Chapter 6: Diving Deep

In which life or death is a hell of a lot closer than the new Mrs. Ari Levinsky could possibly imagine.

"Boss? What do you want me to do here?"

Ari was still pacing, watching his bride, sunning herself obliviously on the boat. She was trying to tempt a seagull with a bit of bread and laughing at its antics.

"Boss?"

His gaze switched to the sand dune where he could just see the glint of sunlight off the rifle aimed at the boat. Ari shook his head. He was fucking second-guessing himself? Really? *What the fuck, Levinsky*, he snarled internally, *nut up!*

Looking back at the boat, he watched Heather gingerly adjust herself on the seat. Yeah, his girl was sore after that pounding he gave her perfect little cunt that morning.

"Boss? I'm in position, but the wind's starting to shift-"

"Abort," Ari ground out. "Tell Asim to hold up, I'm going out with them."

"Uh, yes sir."

Ending the connection, he put his phone in his pocket, pacing back and forth. He'd wait a little longer. Howard, a former CIA agent and currently on his payroll was still doing some digging around. He could wait.

His sweet little bride looked up and smiled to see him hop on the deck before their captain took off. "You're coming with us after all?"

"Yeah," he kissed her hard, squeezing her ass a little. "My business got done sooner than I thought."

***

The dive boat was heading for a spectacular natural formation - a massive, almost perfectly round depression in the ocean floor that dropped from twenty feet to one hundred and thirty, turning the water from a vivid blue-green to a deep sapphire. It was such a startling difference that it was easily visible as the boat approached it.

"Once you have proved yourselves on the descent," Asim said, "there is a ring of beautiful coral reefs near the edge of the depression. There's all kinds of fish and other sea life you won't see anywhere else."

"Amazing..." Heather sighed happily. She caught Ari looking at her with an indulgent little smile, he'd seemed a little weird that morning, so it was nice to see him back to his loud, profanity-laden self.

"Let's dive this bitch!" he shouted, hauling on his tanks and heading over to help Heather with her's, brushing Asim away. "You ready, baby?"

She laughed, so excited that she kissed him back when his lips came down to maul her before letting her put in the mouthpiece, even giving him a saucy little nip on his bearded chin. The growl she got back was deeply alarming. In the best way.

What have I turned into? Falling backward into the water, the new Mrs. Ari Levinsky questioned her sanity.

***

"Hey, Mr. Levinsky, we really need to talk," Howard said, scratching anxiously at his beard, "I have more information that's matching up with what the wedding crashers confessed to, so..." He groaned under his breath, "We should talk before you make any big decisions, okay? Yeah, thanks. I'll just be here..." He hung up, turning his office chair to look at the Manhattan skyline, "...hoping you don't fuck this up, Levinsky."

***

Heather noticed that her lecherous new husband was following very closely as she started the descent into the crater, he was focused more on her than the wonders hiding in the sapphire hue. She felt his gloved hands on her hips, a brazen squeeze of her left breast under the wetsuit and at one point, jostling her oxygen tank. *Perv...* she thought, grinning around her mouthpiece.

Keeping an eye on her regulator, Heather squee'd silently to see that she'd dropped to over 100 feet, the deepest dive she'd ever accomplished. There was a silvery-purple eel or something darting in and out of the darkness and she was swimming toward his flashing tail when she realized the oxygen flow from the tank was gone. Seizing the SPG gauge, her chest heaved. *Zero? Zero freaking oxygen?* Heather thought frantically, *There was no way! I checked it myself in the boat!* Swimming in a circle, she tried to spot Ari. The spotlight on her BC bounced back and forth, skittering through the dark water and finding no sign.

So, no one could blame Heather for the full-throated scream she let out as she was grabbed from behind, precious bubbles of air escaping her mouth. But a giant hand drew a regulator to her mouth, forcing her to take a breath. Then her monolith of a husband was staring at her, watching her wide teary eyes through her mask. She started her ascent, Ari's big body wrapped protectively around hers.

"What the fuck happened, Heather?" He was already shouting as she broke the surface of the water, all red-faced and furious-looking.

"I don't know, I-" she was shaking again and held up her useless gauge, "I ran out of oxygen, the sensor alarm didn't come on- I don't get it! I checked my tanks on the boat, I always do-" She was being hauled briskly out of the water as if she and all her scuba gear weighed no more than a starfish, and then she was on Ari's lap as he soothed her.

"It's okay, bunny," his heated body surrounded Heather, all that warm skin feeling so comforting on her chilled arms and legs. "Fuckin' tanks. I'm gonna buy Asim all new gear. This is bullshit." Had her face not been buried in his hairy chest, she might have seen the boat captain roll his eyes elaborately at her spouse as he turned away.

After her shaking died down and she was feeling warm and comfortable again, her cheek against his chest started vibrating along with his loud voice. "You know what you need, honey? We're just gonna snorkel for a while. You can see some amazing shit in these reefs!"

Part of Heather wanted to get back on dry land, to just sit for a minute and think about what happened. But the other half - *the lower half* - her snarky inner voice noted, that the brilliant sun and clear blue sky made for perfect viewing conditions in the water. No tanks to weigh them down this time. And also, that Ari's giant hand was stroking the inside of her thigh and her lady garden was suddenly eager to bloom. Knowing that the man had no problem defiling her in front of an audience, maybe the water would provide some cover.

Swimming through the exquisite coral reef - fiery shades of red and orange, blinding bursts of pink and aqua - was a lot like being chased by a sea lion. Every time Heather slowed to look at a delicate coral arrangement or an elaborate little fish, the looming shadow of Ari Levinsky, Newlywed and Massive Pervert, was right on top of her.

"Look at you in this bikini, pretty girl..." his gaze was avid, greedy and part of her couldn't help being turned on that this colossal man seemed constantly aroused by her. That he couldn't keep those gargantuan paws of his off her body. He'd already peeled her wetsuit off on the boat and she was reduced to her bright pink two-piece, which seemed to be slipping from the body parts it was meant to cover.

There was something about where they were; the buoyancy of the salt water, the waves were gentle, the coral surrounding them protecting their bodies from the harsher movements of the ocean. The water was crystal clear and looking down, Heather could see the front of this enormous lunatic's swim trunks were already tenting ominously.

"Uh, Ari…" He was creeping up behind her now, a huge shadow over the sunlit coral, just like the finned predator he reminded her of. "Um, the boat's right there," she mentioned, anxiously eyeing the vessel anchored off the shallow reef.

Asim and the rest of the crew were busy coiling rope, mopping the decks and other boat-type activities. No one was looking in their direction, but it's not like the two of them weren't sitting in the middle of a brightly colored bed of coral and really, really visible. His arms slid around her, one giant bicep bunching up comfortably by her breast. The heat of her massive spouse really was something, radiating off his hairy chest and sculpted pectorals, making the tender skin of her neck and back feel like it was scorching.

"The crew can totally, uh…" His long fingers were kneading her breasts, slipping under her bikini top. "Um…" What was she trying to say again?

Ari's chuckle was low, filthy-sounding like he'd just told her the punchline to a dirty joke. "Do you want them to see you, baby? That sound interesting? A good girl like my Heather getting railed while everyone on that boat is watching and wishing they were me?" One muscled forearm went under her breasts while the other started inching down her bottoms, his hardening cock pushing gently against the soft globes of her behind.

Heather shook her head. Nope. Nope, nope, nope, she did not have an exhibitionist kink and no, she did not want the nice captain of their dive boat enjoying the live show that apparently Ari had in mind. Her head must have been shaking fast enough to fly off her neck because her heartless spouse put his hand on her jaw, turning her face to kiss him.

"No, bunny?"

Heather's muffled, "Uh-uh!" made him laugh, and his beard tickled her skin as he whispered in her ear, "Then you better be real quiet, honey. A nice girl like you..." He effortlessly manipulated her body into facing the other direction, shielded by his broad shoulders as he lifted her up, pushing a thigh between hers and running two calloused fingers up and down her center. His chin was resting on her shoulder as he watched her thighs shake, trying to not move too much as his hand delved between them.

But then that beautiful lunatic had the nerve to pull his fingers from her, holding them up, rubbing his thumb and forefinger together, the slick on them glistening in the sunlight. Heather stifled another groan as Ari put them in his mouth. "Mmm," he said appreciatively, "sweet and salty."

That's it. I am going to die, Heather thought dimly. *I survived the shootout that was my wedding day only to die on a coral reef on the other side of the world because my new husband finally sexed me to death. And I thought Dad's wake was a cluster? Imagine what the poor minister will say at mine?*

Smoothing a massive hand down the soft skin of her stomach, Ari's chest rumbled as she started giggling. "What's so funny?"

"I was um..." Heather tried to quell the giggles but they kept rising from her like bubbles, "I was coming to the conclusion that you probably could kill me with-"

His hand slid up to her throat. "What did you say?" His deep voice was sharper now.

She froze, her well-honed survival instincts taking over. "I was... just, uh, joking? That you could k-kill me with sex? Just joking, god I really don't want to go out that way, that really-" Heather was babbling now and he stopped her with a firm kiss, fingers holding her mouth against his.

"Now you're gettin' all demanding," he growled, an odd, teasing tone creeping in to that rumble, "I can't fuck you in front of Asim and his crew, and now I can't fuck you to death? I thought you were gonna be my sweet, obedient little bride?" He didn't even give her a chance to get indignant by pulling down his swim trunks enough to pull that jumbo-sized cock out and slipping it between her thighs, nudging her clit. "Well, okay on those two things, but..." Her breath hitched as Ari pushed himself inside her, an inch at a time, lazily. "I am gonna fuck you. So why don't you just admire the view, babe?"

Heather tried to admire the view, she really, really tried. After all, she was in paradise with the vivid blues and greens around her and the silver flashes of the fish playing in the water around their feet. But that diabolical giant was sliding so slowly inside her, not the greedy pounding that she'd come to expect and mind you, she never complained before because he could wring an orgasm out of her every time. But this... so slow, and spreading her and splitting her wide open, making her legs shake as she curled one around his tree trunk of a leg.

"There it is," Ari growled approvingly, "tightest, hottest pussy I ever pushed into, and all mine, aren't you?"

Licking her lips, Heather tried to remember what he just said, it was a question or something she was probably meant to answer but all she could feel was the thick, heated tip of his cock pushing hard against the front of her channel and his huge, calloused hand on her stomach, pushing in.

One of her hands flailed, trying to find something to grab on to, something to anchor herself but then he was putting her palm between his and her abdomen and oh, my god, she *felt it*. The Prodigious Dick of Ari Levinsky, Mobster and Sex God could actually be felt pushing inside her.

With something that sounded like a cross between a wheeze and a meow, she came.

But he continued on, whispering filthy, complimentary things to her as he moved painfully slow, one gentle slip and slide at a time while his finger circled her clit. Softly. And damn him, at a snail's pace, not letting her come again but keeping her so close to the edge that she could see that monsoon of an orgasm sweeping across the horizon but not close enough to reach it.

And as the sun sparkled down on the water and a light breeze cooled her sweaty forehead, Ari's maddening patience continued until all feeling had left her legs and the only thing she could possibly focus on was the effortless slide of him inside her.

"It's time, Heather," he crooned, "time to come like a good girl. But unless you want them to hear, you gotta keep those pretty lips zipped. Because you can make a helluva racket when you're getting off." She stiffened in indignation and heard a deep groan from behind her as it squeezed his cock motionless in her channel. "Bunny, no more teasing, I swear. Just loosen up and come for me. C'mon... I got you."

She nearly bit her tongue off, trying to keep from screaming as he filled her with heat and her channel convulsed, squeezing his shaft harder. But when his knees gave out and they both sank into the surf, Heather was filled with a sense of power. The first she'd had in this deeply dysfunctional sham of a marriage. And she liked it.

***

Heading back to the shore, Heather fell into a light doze and Ari rolled his eyes at Asim's wink. Tightening the towel around his sleeping girl, he hoped Howard had better news for him, because he really did not want to have to kill his bride.

Chapter 7: Uncle Ivan and the Terrible Dilemma

In which Ari just can't make up his mind about killing his bride.

The dinner guests Ari had told Heather about were so obviously made men that she wished she could raid the buffet and sneak back to their little honeymoon cabana. But no, her husband had taken the entire dining room at the resort's restaurant to wine and dine these terribly unpleasant-looking men.

The group was an odd mix of Somali gangsters and European mafioso and the array of fashion choices was her only real entertainment for the evening. Other women were there, a few well-armed ones who looked far more terrifying than the men, a couple of wives, and some ladies obviously rented for the occasion. Many of the latter looked at Ari covetously, flapping their false lashes like deranged lunar moths. She'd played hostess for her dad on occasion when he was in between wives, so she knew how to smile and keep the conversation at surface level. When it was time for the hoodlums there to plan something vile with her colossal spouse, Heather smiled demurely and started guiding the wives and dates into another room.

"Malen'kiy golub'!"

She knew that voice, turning with arms out, "Dyadya Vanya!"

The rotund gent in a $1,200 tracksuit lifted Heather up in a hug. There was an abrupt displacement of air and Ari was there, gripping her arm and pulling her smoothly away.

"How the fuck are you, Ivan? Glad you could make it! Like your new jet! How do you know my wife, motherfucker?"

The Russian chuckled, "Still the same charming bastard, I see. I apologize for my late arrival, I had a spot of business in Pretoria that ran long. And," he put his arm around her shoulders, hugging her lightly in what was clearly a death wish, "I know your lovely bride because she is family."

Yes, it was true that she was being hugged by a man who was not him, but Ari's expression had been less enraged when he was lighting up the ballroom of the Four Seasons with an AK-47 during their wedding reception.

"Ari?" Heather ventured, "Your... uh, your guests are kind of shuffling around over there. Do you want me to take the ladies somewhere else?"

He lifted her body from the same airspace containing the still-amused Russian and set her down on his other side, the bulk of him blocking out the rest of the room. And then her lunatic husband did the oddest thing: putting his giant paw on her cheek, stroking up and down her throat with his thumb, pressing against her fluttering pulse for a moment. When his gaze rose to Heather's again, they were blank. Like the sharks they'd seen that day during the dive.

"Yeah, baby. That'd be great."

***

They'd finally bid goodnight to their mostly drunk guests in the early hours of the morning and yawning, Heather followed Ari back to their lovely cabana over the water. She was half terrified and half hopeful that he'd want to have sex, but his broad back was turned from her as he looked over some messages on his phone. Sliding into the bathroom, she wearily changed and washed her face.

"So, it seemed like tonight went well," she ventured, rubbing some aloe gel on a couple of spots toasted a little extra by the sun that day. "You know?" Walking into the bedroom, she stopped short. Her new husband was standing, shirtless and his belt wrapped around each big fist, the leather straining between them. "Wh- are you okay?"

"Huh?" Ari blinked, looking a little surprised. "Just thinking. So how do you know Sidorov? Well enough to call him Uncle Ivan?"

"Oh," Heather skirted him and walked to the far side of the bed, putting her phone and a bottle of water on the bedside table. "He's not really my uncle, but I've known him since college." Behind her, his grip pulled on the belt, making the leather creak. "I used to visit his family when I spent that year in Moscow."

***

Ari's massive fists tightened on what was about to be the murder weapon for his wife. Her back was still to him, prattling on innocently about her fucking Uncle Ivan.

Uncle Ivan, who has very strong connections to the Serbian gang that shot up his wedding and offed Andrew Stanfield. If they'd gotten him, too, it would have been one hell of a clean sweep for sweet little Heather.

As it turns out, they hadn't killed all the assassins who'd stormed the ballroom at the Four Seasons. Two of them were left in a warehouse he owned in Jersey. Well, what was left of them. There were some pieces missing, but they were tough, he had to give them that. It took a week to finally get them to spill about who sent them. And their orders to take out him, Andrew, and all their lieutenants. The Stanković Trijada made one hell of a mess at his wedding, but those Serbian motherfuckers didn't get him.

A muscle ticked in his jaw as he ground his teeth, mentally going backward and forward on his girl. Was she involved, was she a pawn? He'd gotten Howard on the phone after the dive.

Earlier...

"I think you might want to hold off, Ari." Howard was rubbing his eyes, it was 3:36am in Manhattan but only a man with a death wish didn't pick up when Ari Levinsky placed a call. "I don't have anything conclusive about your wife having enough contact with the Stanković Trijada to have called the hit. And there's another interesting development."

"What, Howard? Don't give me any more of this 'I dunno' bullshit. You're getting paid to get me specific intel, not this half-assed shit." Ari was pacing back and forth on the pier outside of his honeymoon cabana while his soon to be dead - possibly - bride was showering, singing something about "Rain on Me" and sounding pretty happy.

He heard a slight groan as his man in New York City got out of bed. "I know you were holding off on taking control of Stanfield's empire for the minimal mourning period, but they've been making moves."

Ari's massive fist crushed the beer bottle he was holding. "What the fuck are you talking about?" he snarled, shaking the glass shards from his hand, "What moves? Who's giving the orders?"

What Howard told him was apparently stunning enough to render the colossal blond completely silent, his face growing red as he ground his teeth into calcium powder.

"-Okay?"

Blinking, Ari realized his wife was standing close to him, head tipped up to look higher than his collarbone, which was pretty much where the top of her head reached. She was wearing some little silky green thing that looked like it could tear off pretty easy. "Uh... what did you say, babe?"

Her pretty eyes traveled from his face down to the belt currently being tortured in his giant mitts. "I just... are you okay? Everything went all right, didn't it?"

"Yeah, bunny, it was good." Ari intended to run one finger down that thin strap holding up the top of her little nightie thing, but he realized he was still gripping his belt.

Heather's gaze was now fixed on his fists, the leather straining.

"What... is there something wrong with your belt?"

Groaning internally as his cock officially became the boss of him, he chuckled, letting go of one end and giving it a little snap, the sound of the belt cracking making his pretty, pretty girl jump a little.

"What I'm gonna do with the belt..." Ari grinned, beginning to herd her in the direction of the bed, "...is tie your hands to the headboard so you can't move and I'm gonna eat you out until you come three times. Then I'm going to perch you on my cock and slap that sweet little ass with my belt until you ride me. How about that, baby?"

She'd just hit the bed with the back of her legs and tumbled onto the mattress. "I- oh, my god, you really are going to kill me with sex, aren't you?"

Ari had never felt more desperate to shove his dick into a woman as much as he wanted to with his bride, and he growled, low and dangerous, watching his sweet little Heather shiver again. "Only if you're lucky."

***

Much later, when she still wasn't speaking in full sentences and a lot of mushy-sounding vowels seemed to be all she could utter, her diabolical spouse rose and strolled his magnificent, naked self into the bathroom and started the big tub that looked out over the ocean.

"Aw, bunny, look at you," Ari's giant form bent over her weak, depleted form and easily lifted her out of bed. "You're like one of those boneless chickens or something," he chuckled heartily, the hair on his chest tickling her cheek.

"Vvverrry fun. Ny. Ash...hole," Heather managed as he dropped her into the water (fortunately, not from his full height) and climbed in behind her.

It was so nice... she *was* boneless, it seemed, and lying against his giant chest was oddly soothing. It was so wide, and she could feel the steady beat of his heart thumping against the thin skin of her temple as calloused hands moved the soft, honey-scented soap up and down her arms.

Ari paused to pour her a glass of juice and held it to her lips. It was a sweet gesture, right until she choked on a swallow as his soapy fingers slipped to her center. He paused his defiling of Heather to pat her back, making it feel like he'd dislodged her kidneys but at least the juice didn't choke her to death.

She was dozing lightly in the warm water until he said, "You talked to your stepmother since the funeral?"

"Huh?" Clumsily rubbing her eyes, Heather tried to concentrate. "Candy? No, they whisked her away pretty quick when she fainted and knocked over that huge portrait of Dad at the funeral luncheon."

"Hmm…" he rumbled, "how did she and Andrew get together? Didn't you introduce them or something?"

Heather wanted to burst into deeply ironic laughter, but the only thing that came out was a gurgle. "Not exactly. We went to high school together; she was right before me in the processional because we were in alphabetical order. He got there just in time to see me get my diploma and I noticed he took a picture of Candy first. We were standing together when he came over to see me and he couldn't take his eyes off her. They were married before I even started my first year at the Sorbonne."

Ari jostled her head some more as he laughed. "So if someone hadn't lined you up in alphabetical order, Candy would probably be starring in a rap video wearing a bikini instead of living it up as the Widow Stanfield?"

"Don't be mean," Heather chided sleepily, "I think she really cared about Dad."

"Huh," he said, circling her nipples with his thumbs. "So, what was her maiden name that put her in front of you for the Big Walk?"

Yawning, she managed to say, "Stanković. That's how I met Uncle Ivan. He's really her uncle, not mine."

***

The rest of the honeymoon passed in a sex-fueled blur, and there were a couple of days where the blond Titan she'd married was off doing some Mafioso-type thing because she was too weak to get out of bed. Heather knew his Lear jet took off a couple of times from the private airstrip loaded up with something and returning empty. But she never asked. Candy wasn't the only one who knew curiosity was a very bad trait.

"Hey, baby…"

Heather pulled down her sunglasses and smiled up at Ari, whose gargantuan body was casting a shadow over her and most of their cabana. She was stretched out on the comfy lounge on the deck, pretending to read and really, just trying to rest up for the next time he started mauling her. "Hey, what's up?"

"I'm gonna take the jet and head up the coast for a couple of hours. I got a client I'm meeting. He's an asshole and I'm not inviting him here. You know how the warlords get. Somebody puts a curse on somebody else and then all the machetes are flying."

"Yeah…" she said blankly, "that's, uh, awkward."

"Yeah…" he echoed, that enormous hand of his rasping slowly down her throat. "It's the last night of our honeymoon, babe. I got plans." Ari leaned in to take a fairly aggressive nip at her ear, chuckling when she yelped. "So you should rest up."

Heather would have answered him but his tongue was currently exploring her mouth and nothing else was getting said, until he was good and done with her.

But it wasn't until she was walking a little unsteadily into the cabana when she realized there was a problem. Ari's wallet and phone were still on the bathroom counter. Slipping on some beaded sandals, Heather hoofed it for the airstrip, knowing his rage would be incendiary if he took off without them.

But he wasn't there, only a mechanic who was busy drawing the fuel truck up to the jet. Her head tilted, tapping the wallet against her hand. That was weird. The pilot should already be there, running the pre-flight instrument checks and one of her Mob husband's buddies walking around the perimeter. From the direction she'd come, no one on the tarmac would have seen her. When the worker finished fueling the jet, her eyes widened as he looked around and then slipped a canister into the fuselage.

Well, crap.

She was no aviation expert, but this clearly seemed like a deviation from what she'd seen on pre-flight routines before on her dad's jet.

"Hey, babe, did you find-"

Heather spun to find her husband striding down the path. "Yeah," she forced a smile, holding up his phone, "looking for this?"

"Yes! You're a lifesaver, bunny!" Ari cupped the back of her neck and pulled her in for one of his shamelessly long kisses with lots of tongue. "Okay, I gotta go-"

She dug her fingers into his immense biceps, "Oh, honey," she said loudly, "I'm just going to miss you so much! Will you, uh, cuddle me for a minute?"

Yeah, she'd never win any Golden Globes with that performance but his ocean-blue eyes narrowed and his arms wrapped around her, enclosing her completely as he buried his nose in her hair. "What's going on, Heather?" His voice was deeper, more serious and she could see why grown men pissed themselves when Ari was in full Mob King mode.

Standing on tiptoe to peek over his wide shoulder, Heather whispered, "When I got here, there was no one around the jet but the guy fueling it. He put a canister of something in the fuselage. I don't know who he is, but he's definitely not part of your flight crew."

"Motherfucker!" Ari hissed. "Is he still on the tarmac?"

"No," she groaned, "he took the truck and left while we've been talking."

"Manny!" he shouted to one of his bodyguards hurrying to catch up, "Take Heather back to the cabana. No one gets near her."

"Wait- what are you going to-" the Manny guy was trying to pull her away by her elbow without actually yanking her, but Ari was already talking to the two other men.

"C'mon, Mrs. Levinsky," her new bodyguard groaned, and for a minute, Heather actually looked around for Sarah, the Mafia Matriarch, before realizing he meant her. "Mrs. Levinsky," Manny repeated, "your husband's going to cut my dick off if I don't get you out of here safely, so help me out, huh?"

Heather paced back and forth in the cabana. It was useless trying to figure out who'd tampered with the jet. Half the criminal world wanted her gorgeous, lunatic husband dead. But the realization that she, also, could have been on the Lear jet when it exploded or crashed or whatever these idiots planned made her sit down abruptly, knees weak.
"Assassinated on my honeymoon," Heather laughed a little hysterically, "that even beats Dad's grand finale…"
A colossal explosion rattled the windows around her violently and a fireball erupted from the direction of the airfield.

After her first scream, she managed to dial it down and raced out to see Manny frantically talking into his earpiece.
"Is he alive? Is Ari alive?" Heather shook his arm violently but then, over the sand dune came Ari the Apex Predator Levinsky, Badass Mob Boss looking all kinds of irate but unhurt. She was shocked by the wave of relief that swept over her. This guy like… like bought her from her Dad! This tall, handsome psycho killed lots of people! And yet, she was genuinely relieved and even happy that he was still drawing breath.
"Man, my insurance agent's going to lose his shit over this one," he chuckled, reaching Heather and squeezing her behind in what she assumed he thought was a soothing way. "That fucker detonated when we tried to run a scan on the fuselage."
"Is everyone all right?" Heather could not believe how calm this insouciant psycho could be.
"Everyone's alive," Ari said, "for now. That slippery fucker who tampered with my fuckin' jet disappeared, but my guys will find him. Sorry, babe. They're sending a loaner jet up from Mogadishu, so we got a couple hours delay." Both of his ridiculously large

hands were on her butt now, easily encompassing her entire behind. "I'm gonna thank you for saving our asses by riding yours."
Oh, god, Heather moaned internally as he threw her over one
shoulder and headed back into the cabana.

***

The new jet showed up with an alarmingly large diamond pen-
dant that matched Heather's alarmingly large wedding ring. Ari
flipped the black velvet box open. "My girl gets more than just
coming five times for saving our lives," he said casually as she
writhed internally and tried to pretend the ten wiseguys surrounding them didn't hear that. "Or was it six?" A chuckle hastily
disguised as a cough from behind her ended that feeble hope.
Reaching behind her, Ari closed the delicate clasp on the necklace
with surprisingly graceful fingers. "I was looking at something
bigger, but I remembered you like simple stuff. Elegant."
Damn him. This hulking lunatic was worming his way into her
heart.

***

So, when they did land back in New York City, after a long shower,
a nap, and a change of clothes so she'd look Rich, Upper East Side,
Heather walked out with Manny in tow to find the standard sinister black luxury SUV waiting for her. She told them where she
wanted to go, and her new driver and Manny nodded politely.
Walking through the doors of the opulent Chez Stanfield, she
could already see Candy's influence- bubblegum pink curtains in
the living room and a full marble fountain with a naked bronze
mermaid with impressively detailed bronze nipples spouting lav-
ender water installed in the front hall.
Her old classmate/not stepmother was lounging behind the massive mahogany desk where Andrew Stanfield used to make decisions about who to kill, how many billions to swindle, and what
crucial public servants needed their bribe money increased.
"Heather! Hey, girl!" Candy stood to greet her with open arms and

a big, wet smack on her cheek. "How was the honeymoon?" She eyed the constellation of hickeys on Heather's neck and sniggered. "It couldn't have been that good, you're still walking."

Heather rolled her eyes, "Are you kidding? I'm lucky I have any fluids left in my body." Candy was already shoving a flute of champagne in her hand when she stopped her. "Bitch, wasn't Andrew enough? Why did you try to kill Ari? And on my honeymoon? Really?"

Chapter 8: "No, F*ck YOU!"

In which the fighting turns dirty. No holds barred. Who'll come out on top, Heather or Ari?

"I have no idea what you're talking about," Candy said primly, sipping from her glass of champagne.

"Really?" Heather jabbed a finger at her, "Please. The airhead act worked with my dad but you and I know you were a Rhodes Scholar! It didn't even hit me until I ran into Uncle Ivan at the Port Sudan Diving Resort. The guy who tampered with Ari's jet? It took me a while to remember where I'd seen him before. He's one of Ivan's people! You suck!"

Candy didn't even bother to pretend anymore. "Well, you didn't help me out, either, Heather! Ari was a loose end from the wedding - I was gonna take them both out and you would legally be a Levinsky! We would rule the entire East Coast! The Queen Bees, girl!" She shuddered, the fluffy angora of her pink sweater sending gentle little bits of fluff into her champagne. "I earned it. Five years with Andrew! Five. Years!"

Heather scoffed, "Are you remembering the part where the jet exploding could have killed me, too? So it's hard to be the Queen Bee when I'm feeding the crabs at the bottom of the Red Sea!"

"You're overreacting," Candy shifted, waving a hand in an airy fashion as if to dismiss her petty grievances. "Ivan knew it was another one of Ari's business trips. The jet fuel ignites the canister after takeoff. Then, kaboom! Easy peasy. Besides…" she was going on the offensive, Heather knew this Candy, the one from their high school rugby team who'd beat the crap out of their opponents. "Why did you swap tanks with Ari on that dive? For fuck's sake, girl! You're in the deepest part of the fucking Red Sea and he dies from a faulty tank! That shit happens every day!"

Sputtering and nearly beside herself with rage, Heather yelled, "Are you kidding me right now? I was the one who almost died, you idiot! If Ari hadn't been practically on top of me, I would have suffocated! *This* was your plan?"

Candy's heavily lashed eyes narrowed. "See, this is why I didn't bring you in on this venture! I knew you'd get all pissy about it and then nothing would be good enough for you, and-"

Picking up the crystal ice bucket that had held the rather nice Moët & Chandon, Heather dumped it over her stepmother's head. Candy let out a high-pitched squeal that sounded like steam escaping a tea kettle, flapping her hands uselessly. Drinking directly from the bottle, Heather leaned against the desk until she calmed down.

"Real mature, Heather. Real. Mature!" Candy peeled a fake eyelash off her cheek. "I knew you'd be all conflicted, 'cause Andrew was such an asshole, but he's your dad, and shit. But-"

"I knew Dad was an asshole, you asshole!" Heather shouted, "But he was the only - I dunno - asshole I had!"

Candy started laughing in a weird, hiccupping way because she was still trying to get the ice out of her bra. "Well, now you have a brand new, shiny asshole all of your own," she wheezed, "speaking of which, did you get yours bleached for the wedding? That's a thing again. Did Ari check?"

Then, the two of them were on the floor, just howling. They'd try to calm down, look at each other and start laughing again. Finally relaxed enough to drink from the bottle without choking, they passed the Moët & Chandon back and forth.

"I really wish you hadn't killed Dad," she said finally, "but I can certainly see why."

"Girlfriend, he was about to get rid of me. You remember that crazy Venezuelan redhead who stripped down on the dance floor at the Stanfield Foundation bash?"

"Yes?" Heather said before it all came together and she had to hold back a full-body heave. "Oh, my god! He was going to divorce you for her? Oh, my god!"

"No," Candy said, as serious as she had ever seen her. "Andrew was going to kill me. Don't you wonder why the asshole wasn't paying alimony to any of his exes?"

"Oh, yeah..." she felt stupid. Incredibly stupid. "Why did that never occur to me?"

Candy nudged her shoulder companionably. "You were probably focused on all the other awful shit he did."

"Yeah," Heather sighed, "there was a lot of it." Getting to her feet, she pointed a stern finger. "Do not attempt to kill my husband. Again, I mean. Both hits you ordered could have killed *me*. So cut that out and let me see what life is like in the Levinsky Mafia before we decide what to do with Ari."

"Do not tell me you're getting soft on him!" Candy scoffed, "You know he would take you out in a heartbeat if you got complicated."

Why did that thought hurt her more than terrify her?

"I see you've been busy here," she commented as Candy strolled with her, arm in arm to the front door.

"Yeah," she beamed, "remember Eduardo, my massage therapist? He's also an interior decorator. Talk about lucky!"

Eyeing the water spraying vigorously from the mermaid's nipples in the fountain as she turned to leave, Heather nodded. "Yep. A real Renaissance Man. You go, girl."

After returning to Ari's brownstone, there was a fair amount to unpack from Heather's realization and subsequent discussion with the Widow Stanfield, so it took until she heard the familiar bellow of her spouse as he got home to realize something important.

She didn't swap out the tampered air tanks on their dive. She didn't know anything about it at the time.

So... if she didn't, Ari did.

"There she is! How's my baby, huh? You fucking happy to be back home?" Ari was in the doorway, shoulders nearly brushing each side and blocking any escape.

Taking a deep breath, she smiled sweetly, "It's good. Are you hungry? Your chef left dinner for us, I just need to heat it up."

They stared each other down along the shining expanse of the table in the dining room, Heather making sure she was the one to open the bottle of wine and pour it. *No need to make it easy for him,* she thought bitterly.

"So, how's your stepmother?" Ari asked before putting another forkful of ribeye in his mouth.

"She's redecorating," she tried to keep the giggle out of her tone, but his eyebrow went up.

"I gotta hear this," her husband urged, stretching out his massive arms and easily dwarfing that entire corner of the room.

Good god, he's got, like, the wingspan of a bald eagle, she thought, a little distracted as his broad chest swelled. Shaking her head, trying to focus, she told him about the new fountain. Unsurprisingly, Ari thought that was hilarious and roared with laughter while also chiding her for not getting a picture of, "That epic shit."

Yeah, it was a pretty nice dinner, the Levinsky chef had created an amazing combination of buttery-soft steak and scampi, which Ari was tossing into his mouth by the dozen. The house was quiet, Heather knew there were bodyguards somewhere because this was Ari Levinsky, Mob Boss of Manhattan but it felt like just the two of them in their little candle-lit oasis. But by the time she brought in the fluffy chocolate-pistachio eclairs the mood had shifted. She could feel it, thrumming just under her skin, a lifelong instinct to hide or run trying to urge her to *move,* to do something...

"So, honey." Ari was leaning back in his chair, the light catching the scary new tinge of grey seeping over his sunny blue eyes. "So. When were you going to tell me that your Dad wasn't the only target at our wedding?"

Frozen, the plate of eclairs was forgotten in her hand as Heather stared at the stranger at the dining table. After a mere three weeks or so, she thought she knew the man who'd made her marry him. Loud, profane, crass, and occasionally sweet. When he wasn't sexing her half to death.

"Excuse me?" She was suddenly, simply furious. Candy nearly killed her, the sloppy cow and now it looked like this gigantic lunatic was going to finish the job. "Are you remembering that I got yanked up by the hair with a gun pointed at my head at our reception? You know, the one where you were lighting up the ballroom of the Four Seasons with what- a rocket launcher?"

Heather flinched when Ari made a sudden movement, but he lifted his hand mockingly to show that he was just holding his phone, which he laid on the table, pressing the speaker button. The audio was crackling, muffled occasionally by something that sounded like hair brushing over the speaker.

"Heather! Hey, girl!" There was a big, wet smacking sound, Candy kissing her cheek, she remembered. "How was the honeymoon?"

She was shaking like a leaf in a windstorm, she knew what was coming next. "Are you kidding? I'm lucky I have any fluids left in my body." The clinking of glasses, and then, the words Heather had intended to take to her grave. "Bitch, wasn't Andrew enough? Why did you try to kill Ari? And on my honeymoon? Really?"

The audio fuzzed, volume rising and falling and ending with a click.

Heather was on fire. "You bugged me? You *asshole!*"

The plate containing the regrettably delicious-looking eclairs was sailing across the table and smashing against Ari's raised hand, spraying him with tasty pistachio filling and china shards.

And she was out of the dining room and racing down the hall.

Heather could hear his thundering footsteps shaking the shining wooden floors as Ari caught up with her by the door of his office- a large and stately room filled with all kinds of impressive, CEO-type stuff that she was sure her husband had never touched. But an old school executive palace like that? A letter opener... a brass paperweight... she was going to disable this colossal lunatic before he finished her off.

"Get off me, you psycho!" Heather kicked at him furiously as Ari laughed - a mean laugh, filled with dark intent and scary. Leaning over, he drove a giant shoulder into her midsection and straightened, carrying her into the office like a bag of flour and shoving the heavy door shut behind him. She heard the finality of the heavy "thunk!" - the weighted menace of a soundproofed room. His massive deltoid muscle was digging painfully into her abdomen, one arm firmly against the back of her thighs to keep her from kicking him.

"No can do, baby. We're gonna have a little talk." Ari flipped her over briskly, dumping her on the desk on her ass and shoving her back with a hand between her breasts. "And since the only time you can't fake it is in bed, I'm gonna fuck the truth out of you."

"Fuck you, Ari!" Heather hissed, so furious that she almost felt like it was setting her aflame, though that could have been from this gigantic lunatic's calloused hands, briskly pulling her thighs apart. When she continued thrashing like a deranged eel, he growled, yanking off his tie and quickly lassoed her hands and tied them to the corner of the desk.

Ari rose up over her, huge and intimidating as hell, planting his hands on either side of her head. "No, bunny, fuck *you*."

And it was on.

Flipping Heather over onto her stomach, Ari ripped off her undies at the same time, slotting between her legs and one hand holding her ankles linked just over his ass. She discovered that she was wet, embarrassingly slippery and his first thrust was made easier than it should have been. Yelping, she twisted at the belt binding her wrists, trying to get loose so she could slap at him, get him out of her so she could think - fight him somehow - but his second foray inside her blew that plan out of the water.

The sheer weight of him, the size of his cock felt even bigger in this position and she yelped again as it smashed against her cervix.

The memory of Candy's crass and misspelled note about "Beating your curvix like a dusty rug," rose and it was everything she could do to not start giggling uncontrollably. Because she needed to catch her breath and it didn't seem like this gargantuan dickhead was slowing down anytime soon.

The way her legs were tangled behind his back made Heather's back arch, made that stupidly talented cock of his push brazenly past where any polite male organ was meant to go. Ari was poking around in all sorts of places and every time he bottomed out in her, there was another bright flash of pleasure/pain.

Ari chuckled breathlessly, a bit of blond hair falling into his eyes. He'd taken her chin and turned her - twisted uncomfortably - to look at him. "Oh, bunny. Being scared turns you on, doesn't it? Don't lie, you're making a puddle on my desk."

Horrified, Heather tried to look down but the angle was impossible. Yanking her chin from his grasp, she gripped on to the other end of the desk, trying not to scream. This beefy lunatic had her pinned in a way where most of her weight was on her center, which was pressed against the blunted edge of the desk, rubbing against her clit. The extra pressure was maddening and it took everything she had to not come and give him the satisfaction.

"I sw- sw- swear to god Ari, when I get loose, I'm going to..." She broke off, gritting her teeth. She was so close, so freaking close and the way his cock was driving into her made it impossible to stop and...

Pulling out of her, Ari effortlessly flipped Heather over again, yanking her bound hands loose from the desk and forcing her to balance on them as he put her feet on the other edge of the smeared surface, hauling her up by her hips. She was panting, furious and sweaty, giving him a death stare that was eerily reminiscent of Andrew's. "Aw, shit bunny. Were you about to come?" he asked solicitously, "Sorry." Resting just the wide head of his cock inside her channel, her complete asshole of a husband rotated his hips. "Anything you wanna tell me?"

"Go to hell, you complete asshole of a husb-"

"No?" he interrupted, "Okay." His hips snapped forward and he

64

drove that prodigious shaft right back inside her and this time, her yelp turned into a screech. Ari was looking down at where the two of them were joined together and she just hated that look he got; turned on, self-satisfied, greedy, proud. Wait, when did she get to know this mob boss well enough to recognize his expressions? He was sweating, too, his huge chest shiny, that perfectly defined six pack rippling. His shirt was yanked open and half off one arm, pants around his ankles.

"Goddamn, Heather," he groaned, "I'm gonna keep fucking you and you aren't comin' until you talk, so you just keep giving me that Princess Death Stare." Ari shifted his hips, swiveling them in some insane way that sent his cock driving hard against the front of her, flicking a calloused thumb against her already overtaxed pearl.

The muscles in her thighs were tightening and a thin whine escaped her clenched teeth. She was *not* giving in to this bastard, she was not...

"GOD-damnit!" Heather screamed as he abruptly fell back into his big leather chair, big hands sliding up to her shoulder blades to haul her along with him. She was face to face with this... this towering, heartless, stupidly gorgeous asshole she'd been forced to marry. As her eyes narrowed furiously, his fingers curled up over her shoulders, back arching to put her breasts right at his stupid, perfect red lips.

Ari suckled one nipple, and then the other, nibbling, circling them with his agile tongue and then he reared back and buried his face between her breasts, groaning with pleasure. "These perfect tits," he rasped, "I could play with 'em all night." But it seemed his moment of reflection was over because his hips shot up, nearly knocking Heather over and off his cock before he pulled her back down.

She'd admired his ass before, appreciated those perfectly structured muscles in his thighs - particularly when he made her ride them - but her awareness of her husband's sheer strength was newly awakened as his hips kept thrusting up, bouncing her like a beach ball. As Heather came back down each time and all of Ari was buried inside her, he'd give her severely overtaxed pearl a little slap. She'd screech with indignation and he'd do it again.

At this point, she was beginning to feel like the boneless chicken he'd once compared her to, breasts bouncing wildly out of her dress, which was yanked down around her waist. Her legs were slung over the leather-covered arms of his chair, and that squeaking sound she was hearing was apparently their combined sweat and slick making a mess of his once-pristine Bernhardt Marco swivel chair.

"That's good quality," Heather mumbled absently, trying to focus on the finer points of leather seating to avoid the fact that her orgasm was barreling down on her. Her very toes were pointing helplessly and those maddening little slaps from Ari's fingertips were really becoming impossible to ignore.

It was his triumphant laughter that brought her back into full awareness of her plight. "You wanna come, bunny," he leered, "I can feel you starting that little wiggle you do with your hips. Tell me what I want to know. Did you set up that ambush at our wedding with your psycho stepmom? Were you gonna take us both out?"

"She- She's not my st- stepmom, asshole!" He was bouncing Heather so vigorously now that she was sure she was going to come. He couldn't stop her, screw Ari, she was just going to...

Okay, now Heather started screaming because he stopped *again.* That no-good son of a bitch bastard face stopped, yanking out of her and making her feel the ache of being empty. Who knew that her lady garden, clenching on nothing, hips circling trying to find him again, that it could feel more painful than being stuffed full of Ari the Complete Asshole Levinsky?

"What was the plan, Heather?" His voice was colder now. She wouldn't have characterized his earlier behavior as playful, but next to this tone? This sounded like Mob Boss Levinsky, the guy who burned down warehouses and made bodies sink to the bottom of the Hudson River.

"I don't know what you think you know," Heather hissed, batting fruitlessly at him, "but whatever it is, you're wrong! I got dragged home from my graduation trip so Dad could marry me off to you! Then, there's guns and stuff blowing up and *aaah!* Just let me come!"

Perversely, Ari seemed pleased by her tantrum. "Not just yet, bunny," he soothed, "because you knew something when you went to visit Candy today."

Heather was staring at his cock. Never a dick, or a prick, or a penis. This was a cock, a gigantic, perfectly-shaped, marble-hard cock. It was shiny and slick and it looked just as good as she already knew it felt. Shaking her head, she tried to force her few remaining brain cells to maybe knock together and fire off a synapse or two. "Well…" her brows drew together. "So did you! You knew when you were asking me about Uncle Ivan, didn't you?" Embarrassingly, she felt her eyes water. "Did you know about this for our entire honeymoon? How?"

Ari must have noticed that revelation dialed back her orgasm, because he began running his thick cock between her wet and swollen lips, the silky tip nudging against her clit. One giant hand moved up to gently squeeze her breasts, the other not-so-gently squeezing her throat. "Not all those bastards died during the shootout. There's a couple of them in one of my warehouses." Horribly, Ari chuckled, "Well, bits and pieces of 'em, anyway. But yeah, the name Stanković came up. Along with their orders to kill me and my top guys."

He must have noticed that she hadn't drawn a breath for a while because his long fingers released their loose grip on her throat, but really, it was from shock. Shock, that this colossal lunatic had known all along. Also, shock that his slip and slide game with her girl parts was winding her up again.

What kind of animal gets turned on when it's caught in the snare? Heather thought, *Me. I am that animal.*

"Well, the order didn't come from me," she said bitterly. "I wish I'd been smart enough, or brave enough. But no, I was just the sucker trying to learn my wedding vows - in *Aramaic* - fifteen minutes before my wedding to a gigantic maniacal mob boss!" She might have been getting a little teary-eyed but the fact that this perplexing asshole looked even more pleased was keeping her from breaking down because she just could not figure him out.

"Aw, bunny," Ari soothed, "you've been such a good girl." He brushed her sweaty hair off her face and smiled down at her tenderly.

There was one quiet moment in the hurricane that was their marriage. One still, gentle moment as they stared at each other. Even with his hair askew and magnificent chest still heaving, Ari Levinsky was still unreasonably gorgeous: full, pink lips in a gentle smile.

And then he threw Heather back on the wreckage of his desk and her legs over his shoulder, holding her thighs together as he pushed that prodigious cock back into her, firing her up and again and it didn't matter that she was still so pissed off at him. She came. Like a rocket, feeling like different parts of her were creating their own little fireworks and it all came together in an incendiary moment and she clamped down on him so hard that Ari actually halted, held tightly inside her as her orgasm forced him into his.

"Holy fuck, bunny!" His voice was a little high, "You're gripping me like a fist- goddamn, I'm-" And then the terrifying Mob Boss of Manhattan came too, flooding her, dripping out of his bride and smearing his desk beyond hope of recovery.

"I never came that hard in my life," Ari wheezed. He'd managed to get Heather off the desk - still attached to his cock - and stumbled over to the couch, kicking off his pants before they tripped him. His face was currently buried between her breasts, huge body half on her and his long legs draped awkwardly over the sofa's arm.

"Uh, huh..." It was the most coherent she was going to be for a while, and she stared up at the ceiling and petted his finely shaped deltoids with one lazy hand.

Wrapping one of her legs more comfortably around his waist, Ari leaned over her. "So what did you say to Candy after the mic shorted out?"

Heather knew she should be pissed off again, righteously so, but she was really tired. "I..." rubbing her eyes, she yawned, "I told her to hold off on killing you. First of all, because the hits she ordered on you kept getting mixed up and nearly taking me out instead."

"And the second reason?" Ari was grinning his stupidly confident grin.

"Huh?"

"The second reason," he gloated, kissing slowly down one side of her neck, "I'm bettin' the second reason is you're liking me."

"No..." Okay, that was the weakest denial ever.

And then, *then* Ari Levinsky had the nerve to smile down at her, looking almost tender. "Ma said you weren't involved. She was sure of it."

Heather angled her head a little, "Why?"

He was laughing, his furred chest rubbing against her in a really distracting way. "Because you saved her dogs. Ma said there was no way you were gonna risk your life to suck up to her by getting those yappy little bastards if you ordered the hit on me."

Okay, now she was giggling and remembering shoving that chicken cutlet from the overturned banquet table up the sleeve of her wedding dress and crawling through the wreckage of the cake to find those irritating bags of fur.

But then something else surfaced in her sex-wrecked memory, and Heather snarled, "Hey, you tried to kill me!"

Ari definitely looked guilty. "I wasn't really gonna strangle you with my belt, I was just all pissed off from the Uncle Ivan thing."

She struggled loose, his cock popping out of her as they shared a groan. "Your belt? I thought you were just being kinky! You were going to strangle me? What the hell, Ari?"

He rubbed his forehead, "Wait. What did you think I did?"

"The tanks!" Heather said accusingly, "Candy had someone tamper with your oxygen tanks on the dive and you swapped them out with mine!"

***

Ari was tired as fuck and his indignant little bride was being kind of cute but still, he was really fucking tired. Then he figured out what she was so mad about. "Your tanks? No, I swapped them out because they had the smaller regulator. They were lighter than yours so I knew you'd be more comfortable."

Heather's pretty face cleared a bit. "Oh. Okay."

And then he fucked it up, big time. "I thought you'd caught sight of the rifle trained on your tanks, or somethin' and-"

She wiggled out from under him and landed on the oriental rug with a thump. Gathering the tattered remains of her dress around her and covering up those spectacular tits, she struggled to her feet. "You were going to *blow me up?* You were really going to-"

"No, bunny, I didn't though, right?" He was up, thick thighs kinda shaky still from getting half his body weight sucked out of his cock and in her tight little cunt. "I couldn't give the order; you were already under my skin and-"

And then she pointed her finger at him and said it. She fucking came right out and said it.

"I'm telling your mother!"

Ari groaned internally, that meant he had the rest of the night to convince his new wife to not spill to Ma and keep her from cutting his dick off.

Heather was halfway out the study door before he caught up, throwing her over his shoulder and heading for the stairway toward the master suite. "Tell her tomorrow, bunny. I'm taking you to bed."

Notes

I spent some time reading over Jewish wedding ceremonies and I sincerely hope I have not insulted anyone. There's direct links included with all the wedding phrases relating to Jewish customs. Thank you!

By the way...

Thank you for sharing Ari and Heather's adventures! If you enjoyed the story, would you mind leaving a review on Amazon.com? Here's an easy-peasy direct link:
Amazon.com/review/create-review?
&asin=B098QXVQ76

Afterword

A sincere and whole-hearted thank you to everyone who has bought *Mr. and Mrs. Ari Levinsky Invite You to... the Worst Wedding Ever* - or any of my books, or read it here on Kindle. Proceeds from the book benefit the two crisis nurseries in my city.

The crisis nurseries here are non-profits who exist to serve families when the parents are overwhelmed and in desperate need of help. They can bring their children there to be safely and lovingly cared for while the parents are plugged into resources to help them - job training, mental health care, housing resources and more.

Before I became a mother, I'm not sure I would have understood fully what it takes for a parent to bring their child in to be cared for by strangers. But I recognize the look now: terror that you might hurt or neglect your little person, shame that you need help, fear that you're being judged. Aching grief.

But! When the parents come back for their kiddos, they look so different. There's joy and relief and most importantly, hope. So thank you for your assistance and generosity in supporting these families with your kind donations.

You can find out more about crisis nurseries, and where to find one - or start one - in your area on my Tumblr page: ariannafraser-writes.tumblr.com

About The Author

Arianna Fraser

Working as an entertainment reporter gives Arianna Fraser plenty of fuel for her imagination when it comes to writing tales about Norse Mythology - Loki in particular - and current-day romance-suspense stories. There will always be an infuriatingly stubborn heroine, an unfairly handsome and cunning hero - or anti-hero - romance, shameless smut, danger, and something will explode or catch on fire. It's clear she is a terrible firebug, which is why her husband  has sixteen fire extinguishers stored throughout the house.

When she's not interviewing superheroes and villains, Arianna lives in the western US with her twin boys, obstreperous little daughter, and her sleep-deprived husband. And like her beloved Loki, she is very fond of snakes.

Have a thought? Wanna share? ariannafraser88@gmail.com

Find her on Tumblr: https://www.tumblr.com/blog/view/ariannafraserwrites
On Goodreads: http://bit.ly/ariannafrasergoodreads

Books By This Author

The Reluctant Bride - A Dark Mafia Romance

Wait. What do you mean, my dad gave me to you?

I was ready for a fresh start in England, a career with the London Symphony Orchestra. But my father's "underperforming" company is bought out by The Corporation. Suddenly, I'm being told I'm marrying the tall and terrifying Thomas Williams, because dad would rather trade me to keep control of his company. Thomas tells me that it "looks better" to be a married man as his organized crime empire starts a partnership with the Russian Bratva Syndicate.

Really?

I'm a wife. I have a giant diamond ring to prove it... and a husband who can be kind in one moment and scary in the next. And there's car chases, and assassination attempts. There's a body in my cello case! Who has a marriage like this?

But by the time we're in St. Petersburg and surrounded by new friends and old enemies, my gorgeous, terrifying husband might just need me.

We might even be... Don't make me say it! There's a slight possibility that we could be falling in love.

The Reluctant Bride is a Dark Mafia Romance and a stand-alone in The Corporation series. It is for 18+ readers only.

The Reluctant Spy: A Dark Mafia Romance

Would you marry the vicious head of an international crime ring to save your family?

When Maura MacLaren is outed as the M:I6 spy sent in to bring down me and The Corporation, it should have cost her everything: including her life and everyone she loves.

But I have a different plan for the woman who managed to trick me.

Under The Corporation's law, the only way I can save her life - and the lives of her family - is to force her to marry me. But as my bride, I'm going to make her pay for what she's done. Maura will be my pretty, submissive little doll.

Because if I'm living with a bruised heart and bruised pride, so is she.

The Reluctant Spy - A Dark Mafia Romance - is a stand-alone book in The Corporation series. It is meant for 18+ readers only.

I Love The Way You Lie: Loki, The God Of Lies And Mischief - A Dark Loki Paranormal Romance

A nameless princess: innocent, damaged and very lethal. A ruthless king with the power of a god. And trouble, lots of it. When King Loki of Asgard takes the daughter of the Dark Elven Queen captive, he not only strips an enemy of a powerful weapon, but gains for himself a wife. Now, the newly named and wed Queen Ingrid must learn to survive the perils of court life, the wages of

war, and most dangerous of all, her seductive husband's bed.
I Love the Way You Lie is a Dark Loki romance for 18+ readers only.

Mr. And Mrs. Ari Levinsky Invite You To... The Worst Wedding Ever - An Arranged Marriage Mafia Romance

Heather's given to Mafia King Ari Levinsky in an arranged marriage to create an alliance with her terrible mobster dad. She's supposed to be touring Europe after graduating from college, but before she can blink, she's standing at the altar trying to read her vows in... Aramaic? Her new husband is gigantic; tall, muscled, terrifying and loud. And she doesn't even get to pick out her own wedding dress! A romantic beach honeymoon, so much double-crossing, and she finally realizes that the only way to outsmart her giant, gorgeous, dangerous husband, is to out-sex him.